CW00496772

Trail of Betrayal

Nicole Simon

Published by Nicole Simon, 2024.

TRAIL OF BETRAYAL

First edition. February 2, 2024.

Copyright © 2024 Nicole Simon.

ISBN: 979-8224649396

Written by Nicole Simon.

Trail of Betrayal
A Western Romance Mystery

By
Nicole Simon

Chapter 1:
Mail Order Bride

Ruby shook out the wash and hung it on the line, the blistering sun beating down on her soft brown hair. She wiped the sweat off her brow with the back of her hand and stared out at the grassy plains and rolling hills.

This was her new life. The one that she had left the northeast for. Ruby smiled. She had barely arrived two nights ago by stagecoach after three jolting, sleepless, back-aching weeks of travel. The stage coachman was an expert, brandishing his weapon on his person and a large rifle that was next to him the entire trip. He had looked her over before grunting his approval, eager to get on the road and deliver her to her destination.

Upon arrival, Ruby learned from the coachman speaking to a man outside of the saloon that full payment was only received if Ruby arrived in one piece. And *alive* in one piece.

Heavy steps across the wooden floorboards of the house caught her attention and she turned to see Tom standing in the doorway. The summer heat seemed to melt away with his arrival and was replaced by a cool, frigid breeze. Tom was pleasant enough, but Ruby had been surprised by his standoffish welcome when they had met, almost to the point that she wondered if the coachman had made a mistake and accidentally dropped her in the wrong town.

Tom watched her like one would watch a newborn calf, careful that it didn't hurt itself but left alone to mature. Ruby had desired love, but more than anything she had wanted a fresh start. Emma, her sister, had left two months prior, and Ruby had followed in her footsteps even though she knew Emma would be worried if she found out. The sisters had lost contact over the weeks with Ruby traveling and Emma before her.

Ruby's arrival late in the night and the two days spent with Tom exploring the ranch had left little to find where her sister may have resided. Tom had casually mentioned she could borrow one of his horses and ride into town. He didn't care much for going into town, he was quick to explain, and he didn't offer to take her or accompany her. Ruby got the feeling that if she wanted to get off the ranch, she was on her own.

Within the short time Ruby had been here in Montana she had already felt that Tom wasn't the one for her. She had read such things about the arranged mail-order bride marriages, and asked around, learning many women broke off the marriage and escaped to greener pastures. Ruby had thought the idea selfish, but now that she was out here in the middle of nowhere, with the once familiar replaced by the unknown, she could see why a woman might change her mind. Still, Emma was here somewhere. Ruby's priorities were to find her sister and reunite with her.

"You can take the bay mare into town tomorrow if you want," Tom called out.

"You sure you don't want to accompany me?" Ruby asked, trying to be polite, but secretly hoping he would say no.

"I'm going to stay here and fix up your room," Tom explained, turning his back on her and heading back into the kitchen.

Ruby's shoulders sagged. *Your room.* Staying in the same room wasn't even a consideration with Tom. Ruby thought she saw admiration in his eyes upon meeting him, but had she been mistaken? Her hand reached up to touch her cheek, wondering momentarily if he had seen something he hadn't liked. There was something about Tom that shut him off from the world and even her. He seemed like a nice enough man, and could maybe even be a friend, but Ruby struggled to see him as anything more than that.

The hot day settled into a cool evening. Ruby's room was at the other end of the meager cabin with a view of the plains. The velvet night sky twinkled with starlight, and Ruby stared up into the dark abyss. The shadows of the evening brought relief along with a drop in the temperature. Ruby lay on her bed with crisp, white sheets and stared into the nothingness. She felt alone, even more so than when she had been back home. She missed her older sister, knowing that she too was out there exploring the world. Ruby wanted to join her. The only reason the tears didn't fall was because of the hope that her sister was nearby. The sliver of the moon smiled down at her and Ruby finally closed her eyes and let sleep take her.

***

Ruby was up with the sun that morning. She quietly shut her bedroom door and padded across the wooden floor to the kitchen, where the fire had already been started and fresh coffee was brewing. She glanced around, but there was no sign of Tom anywhere. She sighed and wondered if he had even slept at all. Standing at the small window, the sun peeked over the rolling hills in the distance, its bright rays slowly stretching forth across the plains to the ranch. Ruby smiled, warmed by the beautiful sight and by the heat of the delicious brown liquid in her mug. She sipped and savored the moment, until a sudden movement outside caught her eye. Tom appeared, leading a beautiful bay mare from the barn, saddled and ready. He tied the horse to the hitching post and checked the rope, patting her gently on the neck.

Butterflies awoke in Ruby's core, studying the man she was supposed to marry. He did have patience and kindness, but he kept his distance and seemed unable or unwilling to make a mental connection with her. A cool morning breeze trickled in under the front door and Ruby shivered. Tom glanced toward the house and Ruby ducked out of sight, hoping he hadn't seen her staring. Tom's well-meaning actions didn't match his clipped tone, and Ruby wondered exactly where she stood with this man.

Heavy steps pounded up the stairs and across the small porch. Ruby moved away from the door, bracing herself for the encounter. Tom opened the door and started, unprepared to see his soon-to-be-bride lurking by the entrance. She guessed he hadn't seen her watching after all.

"Mornin'," he offered with a tilt of both his head and hat. "Hope you slept well."

"Mostly," Ruby admitted. "How about yourself?" she inquired, her voice low and soft.

"Alright," Tom said, and Ruby swore she saw the corner of his mouth lift a little. "The mare is ready when you are. Do you have a gun?"

"A gun?" Ruby asked, lurching backward.

Tom studied her reaction. "I'll take that as a no. Here," he offered, pulling a small pistol out from underneath his coat.

"I don't know how to use one," Ruby stammered, slowly backing away from the weapon.

"You can't travel without it," Tom warned. "All you do is cock this back, aim, and pull. Make sure you point this end at the threat," Tom explained, moving closer. The proximity tightened as did the atmosphere in the house. Tom grew quiet, his eyes locked on Ruby. She saw something there, but what was it. Hope? Guilt? Both?

"Alright," Ruby agreed, thankful that he wouldn't let her leave without protection. She felt safe, flattered almost, but the doubts crept in. Why wouldn't he just go with her? Ruby sighed, fighting the odd feelings in private. This was all so much to process.

"Tuck it in your satchel," Tom instructed.

Ruby nodded and gently laid the gun in the bottom of her satchel and flipped the fringed top over its contents. Tom headed towards the door to hold it open. They crossed the yard, the chickens scurrying about. The mare nickered as they approached.

"This is Bonney. She's good and honest and won't steer you wrong. She knows the way to town and back," Tom explained, reaching for her.

Ruby placed her foot in Tom's cupped hand and he helped her mount the horse. She felt somewhat that he was eager to see her on her way, and the emotions churned within once more.

"I'll be back before dark," Ruby said, and Tom nodded once, looking up at her. Words rose and died on both their tongues. Ruby slowly turned Bonney towards the road, not daring to look back at those brown eyes that followed her.

The road to town from the Morgan ranch was quiet and uneventful but did nothing to stifle the rapid thoughts stirring within Ruby's mind. Would she be able to find Emma? Ruby's heart thundered in her chest. She had so much to see and learn. Especially about the man she would soon call husband, whenever the ceremony and paperwork were to make it official.

Why did Tom keep her at arm's length? She noticed the wolf tattoo on his forearm. Did it symbolize something? Was her to-be husband truly a lone wolf? The questions swirled around in her mind without any hope of an answer. Soon Ruby noticed buildings on the horizon. Horses pulling a wagon crossed in front of them. Ruby pulled on Bonney's reins and halted. A few cowboys sat in front of what could only be a saloon, sipping coffee and watching the town traffic.

Bonney startled, which startled Ruby. She grabbed the reins tighter as another horse of similar color side-swiped past her. Ruby internally cursed, and the other horse stopped and whirled, a rugged cowboy with sky-blue eyes staring back at her. "Best move before you get run over," he quipped, turning his horse, and cantering off. Ruby scowled at his back. Why were the handsome ones always no good? She watched him ride up to the saloon and tie his horse. She bet he was heading in there to drink, even at this early hour.

Ruby patted Bonney, who had already calmed down, and said softly, "Good girl. Let's go explore, shall we?" Bonney moved forward without being nudged and Ruby smiled. Slowly, they meandered through town, a few townsfolks stopping to stare and then whisper. The corners of Ruby's lips turned down. Clearly, some people knew why she was here. Mail-order brides weren't necessarily common, but they were certainly on the rise. More and more young women who were desperate to get out and see the world, to see the Wild West, and find love decided to take the chance.

Some had nothing left, and no one to turn to. They had nothing to lose and everything to gain, so why not? Ruby lifted her chin, ignoring the blatant whispers. A young woman in a light tan bonnet walked cautiously toward the general store. She seemed timid and unsure of herself, Ruby noticed as she observed the stranger, who was similar in age to herself. The woman lifted her eyes as she saw Ruby and gave a smile and small wave. Ruby's heart squeezed with joy. Maybe finding a friend in this nowhere town wouldn't be impossible after all. The woman dipped through the doorway, and several more people soon followed behind her.

At the end of the row of random shops, which included a barber, the general store and saloon, Ruby saw a sign with painted letters, SHERIFF. The wood bowed and splintered, and the rough exterior was in desperate need of repair. The small Sherriff's building faded into the background when Ruby saw the silver star glint in the rising sunlight, and hard eyes boring into her. Ruby gulped and nodded once, turning Bonney into a small circle and heading back down the main street. A woman was animatedly speaking with the Sheriff, and she too stared as Ruby rode by, then leaned in and whispered something. He nodded and spit in the dirt.

Even with the rising temperature of the summer day, the frosty looks chilled Ruby to the bone. This certainly wasn't a very friendly place for a newcomer. The only person who had offered even a tiny bit of kindness had been the young woman going into the general store. Ruby suspected that she had also been a mail-order bride.

She headed back for the saloon, eager to give Bonney a rest and explore on foot. Ruby had never been in a saloon. Surely, it was too early for drunkards and scoundrels to cause any trouble. She tied Bonney next to the brown horse whose rider had nearly crashed into them and headed up the stairs. She pushed open the swinging saloon door and stopped against something hard. An *oof* sound startled her and she saw the cowboy from the road. She had pushed open the door right into him. He stared at her, surprised.

"Best move before you get run over," Ruby smirked, heading for the bar, a slow smile spreading across her face. A low whistle came from behind her, and she could hear a few whispers and remarks. She pulled out a bar stool and sat down, letting her eyes take it all in. The cash register, the barrels on the floor and the lines of bottles on the shelves, full of different colored liquids. A small stage and large mirror, the smell of booze, leather, and morning coffee. The chair next to Ruby scratched across the floor, and the cowboy himself took a seat.

"What are you doing here?" he asked, flashing a devilish smile.

Ruby's head reared back a little. "What are *you* doing here?" she retorted.

"If I answer, will you stop answering with a question?" his handsome blue eyes twinkled as he grinned mischievously.

Ruby quirked a small smile and nodded.

"I'm here to get a coffee, get a drink, and play some cards," he told her. His dimples looked absolutely delightful when he smiled. Ruby tried not to stare but felt herself turning slightly pink.

Ruby cocked her head slightly. "Is that all you do?" She tried to play it cool, but those dimples were definitely having an effect on her.

The man smirked. "Only on my days off." He eyed her, waiting for an answer.

"I'm new here. I'm exploring and looking for someone. My sister, actually. I'm Ruby, by the way," she said.

"I'm Jake," he said as he flashed his gorgeous grin and tipped his hat. His eyes twinkled, and Ruby found herself staring at the mesmerizing pools of sky-blue liquid.

"Who's your sister?" Jake asked, not breaking eye contact.

Ruby blinked and shook her head a little, trying to compose herself. She found herself blushing and heard Jake chuckle. "Emma. Her name is Emma. She arrived here a few months back," Ruby stammered, trying to compose herself. Those eyes and those dimples were an unbeatable combination. It wasn't fair for someone to have both. She struggled to resist his charm.

Jake set his coffee mug down on the bar. He looked at her, and Ruby's stomach tightened.

"What? Do you know her?" she asked worriedly.

Jake looked hard at Ruby, his mouth opening and closing twice. Ruby's heart began to beat faster, a sickening dread rising from nowhere.

"When's the last time you spoke with her?" Jake asked.

Ruby wasn't sure what to make of the question. "A few weeks back, right around the time I left for Montana. She arrived here a few months ago and I decided to follow. We lost touch, with traveling and all," she said nervously, her words hurrying out.

The cowboy continued his stare, and Ruby squirmed. Was it getting hot in here? Her hands felt clammy and she tried to discreetly wipe them on her dress. She tried not to stare at the genetically blessed cowboy. He seemed hesitant to tell her something, and a slow build of panic blossomed in Ruby's core. Finally, he seemed to internally come to some decision, and opened his mouth to speak.

"Emma hasn't been seen in a month," Jake said quietly. "No one can find her," he continued.

Her sharp gasp silenced the bar. Shock and terror washed over Ruby's pretty face, her hands beginning to shake. *How could this be? Could she have run off? No, she would have told me,* Ruby decided.

The panic within reached new heights, and Ruby knew she could no longer sit there. After a few moments more, she stood quickly, the chair tipping over. She marched toward the door, needing to get to air and sunlight, the saloon suddenly much too small and stifling.

"Where are you going?" Jake said, his voice not far behind her.

"To find my sister," she called out.

Chapter 2:
Unveiling Secrets

"Where are you heading?" The handsome cowboy rushed after her, concern filling his deep blue eyes.

Ruby continued marching out past her horse and onto the wide, dusty main street. She strode quickly, her skirt flipping out in front of her as she walked, a sheen of sweat already appearing as the sun began its climb into the sky.

"To the Sheriff," she answered.

Jake scoffed as he caught up to her. "If he knows anything, he ain't sayin'."

Ruby side-eyed Jake and stopped. "And what do you know?" she demanded.

Jake narrowed his eyes. "Only that she went to the city to buy clothes. And didn't return."

"When? Where?" Ruby questioned, her eyes widening.

Jake sighed and turned, moving forward without her.

"You're not going to answer me?" Ruby asked, running to catch up.

Jake shook his head. "Only the Sheriff and your sister might know those details."

Ruby sighed but continued her march ahead. She wondered why Jake wouldn't elaborate, or maybe he couldn't. Maybe that was all he really did know about Emma. The Sheriff and the woman he was speaking to earlier appeared in view. Ruby heard Jake grumble. Her pace slowed as she glimpsed sideways, but Jake wouldn't meet her eyes. The Sheriff and the older woman ceased their conversation as the two approached. The Sheriff's mouth pulled into a frown upon seeing Jake, and Ruby had a feeling she was about to learn more about the cowboy with the dimpled grin.

"Anderson," the Sheriff greeted Jake with a small nod. No warmth, no handshake, and no friendship echoed in the lawman's words. Jake only nodded, standing spreadeagle with his hands on his belt buckle, lifting his chin as if to say *I dare you*.

"Why, Jake Anderson. When did you get back in town?" the older woman asked, a fake smile plastered on her weathered face. Ruby glanced at the Sheriff who was now studying her. The woman merely glanced at Ruby in a once-over look.

"This morning." Jake replied.

"And who's this? A saloon girl?" The woman glanced back at Ruby, a cold glint in her narrowed eyes. Ruby's mouth hung open, stunned by the accusation.

"She's here to find her missing sister," Jake replied, obviously annoyed with the woman's assumption. He looked at Ruby and said, "This here is Rebecca Price, and you'd do well to stay away from this old spider."

Ruby gasped, then tried not to giggle. Rebecca's smile widened, her jet black hair and pale skin indeed giving her a spider-like appearance. Ruby had never seen such ebony-colored hair.

The Sheriff interrupted, irritated by the conversation. "I'm Sheriff Ethan," he greeted with a tip of his hat. "Who's your sister?"

"Emma. She's missing? Do you know anything about it?" Ruby stammered, glad to be back on the subject of her sister.

Sheriff Ethan sighed. "No ma'am. She went to Ash City, about a half a days' stagecoach ride from here to purchase some new clothes. She went alone against Caroline's advice and hasn't been seen since. We do have the law looking for her in Ash City, but haven't heard anything yet."

Ruby's stomach twisted inside. *How could she be missing? Emma? Where are you?* Tears blurred her vision, and the words croaked out. "Who is Caroline?"

Rebecca rolled her eyes at the name, and Ruby decided then and there she wanted nothing to do with Rebecca, even if the women were outnumbered five to one in this town.

"Caroline Baker," The Sheriff smiled. "She knows anything about everything."

Ruby sniffed and out of the corner of her eye saw Jake sidle closer to her.

"Wait, aren't you Tom Morgan's soon-to-be-bride?" Rebecca questioned, her head tilting slightly.

Ruby nodded and felt Jake stiffen at her side. "Yes," she admitted.

"These mail-order brides. They are infesting the town like weeds," Rebecca snarled, glaring at Ruby with new distaste. Jake put his hand on Ruby's shoulder and began to pull her away.

"Better a weed than a shrew," he said back to Rebecca. "Sheriff," Jake tipped his hat in farewell. As Ruby moved forward, whispers tickled her ears. People stopped and stared once more, glancing at Ruby and then Jake and back again.

"Are you really going to get married?" Jake asked.

"I don't know. Not yet anyway. Things aren't what I hoped they'd be. I've been here for a few days. The ceremony was supposed to take place shortly after I got here," said Ruby.

"Isn't that putting the cart before the horse? And why hasn't it taken place yet?" Jake was full of questions. He seemed very interested in her marital status.

Ruby shrugged. "There's something a bit off with Tom. I'm not sure he wants to get married to me."

"Do you want to get married to *him*?" Jake questioned. Ruby shrugged but didn't answer. Bubbly laughter carried on the breeze to both Jake and Ruby. The laughter was contagious, expelled by a female that was obviously in good spirits. Jake groaned again.

"That's Caroline Baker," he said, pointing to a small gathering of people outside the general store.

"I want to speak with her," Ruby said immediately. She left Jake in the dust and headed straight for Caroline, leaving Jake half-running to catch up.

Caroline saw them approach, and the laughter ceased. She bid her gaggle of gossipy women farewell and headed for Ruby, clasping the young woman's hands in hers.

"Oh, for a moment I thought I was looking at Emma," Caroline gushed, her eyes wet with moisture which made them sparkle in the sunlight.

"I'm Ruby. The Sheriff thought maybe you might have information on my sister Emma." Ruby said hopefully. Caroline glanced at Jake and her smile lessened.

"Let's walk and talk, shall we dear? There are too many ears here." Caroline gently released Ruby's hands and they walked side by side in the street, with Jake lingering not far behind.

"What are you doing with Jake Anderson?" Caroline began in a hushed tone.

"What Mr. Anderson does is none of your concern," Ruby answered, shutting down the inquiry and trying to hide her smile. This woman was clearly looking for her next piece of juicy gossip.

"Well then," Caroline huffed, apparently deflated at not getting anything to dish about later. "So, yes, about Emma, your sister. You two look so much alike, I must say. She went to Ash City to shop. I told her that traveling in the coach alone is asking for trouble. The driver was a fill-in, not the usual, and he wasn't even armed." Jake scoffed behind him, displeased with the information. Caroline continued. "She was supposed to return by sundown, but word was sent that the coach hadn't left Ash City because no one could find Emma."

Ruby sniffed, her gut wrenching. The tears formed again and she struggled to hold them in.

"Oh, you poor dear," Caroline said, taking Ruby's hand and patting it. "Someone somewhere must know something, and we'll find out who or what that is, don't you worry." Ruby could only nod, and Jake now took his place at Ruby's free side.

"Where's this fill-in coachman?" Jake asked.

"He's still in Ash City. The Sheriff is going to question him soon though." Caroline opened her mouth and closed it once more. Both Jake and Ruby sensed the internal conflict Caroline struggled with, but Jake beat Ruby in speaking first.

"Spit it out Caroline," Jake growled.

Caroline gulped and shot him a dirty look. In a quiet voice she said, "Well, you know this isn't the first disappearance, which of course has some people talkin' around here. A young man and another young woman about your age," Caroline nodded towards Ruby, "disappeared a few months ago. They were merely passing through, and we had word of their impending arrival, but neither showed up after they had departed the town a few miles from here. I asked around and no one knew what happened to them." Caroline's eyes darted around, landing on Rebecca Price now strolling down the sidewalk with an affluent looking man.

"No one has seen them since they left the last town on their way here?" Ruby repeated. Caroline only nodded, her eyes fastened on Rebecca. "Who is that man?" Ruby asked, following Caroline's line of sight.

"That's Mayor Samuel Carter," Caroline said. Jake groaned yet again. "And just between us, Ruby, those two are always up to something."

Jake's eyes narrowed as he too watched the Mayor and Rebecca Price stroll arm in arm.

"The spider and the web-spinner," Jake mumbled. Ruby wondered which was which.

Caroline giggled at that. Rebecca's attention turned towards the sound, and Caroline stood straighter. "Use caution Ruby," she whispered, beckoning towards the two figures that vanished inside the general store. She glanced at Jake and smirked. "And watch out for him too."

Jake only grinned and turned towards the saloon. "I don't like cobwebs and I kill every spider I see," he called back to the two women. Caroline shuffled off to a new gaggle on the sidewalk and was greeted with a warm welcome. Jake glanced back once and jerked his head towards the saloon. Ruby stood momentarily, feeling lost, torn, and crushed by the information, the new surroundings, and the loss of her sister. Quietly, she followed the cowboy back into the bar, knowing there was sure to be gossip about them.

Chapter 3:
A Troubled Past

"Where's Lieutenant Anderson?"

"Late. Our orders are to move forward, He'll catch up."

"Through the canyon? That's known as Native territory."

"There's been no attacks in six months Corporal. Now git."

The small parade of Army soldiers steered their mounts through the sand of Gold Canyon. The walls rose above them, the sun's rays momentarily blocked. The young Corporal shaded his eyes and stared at a spot on top of the canyon wall. A figure appeared. Or did it? The Corporal squinted, the shadows of the canyon playing tricks on his mind and sight. Brush along the top of the walls waved in the breeze that favored the top of the canyon, leaving its innards to swelter in the heat.

Hoof beats off in the distance caught the Corporal's attention and he turned his horse back.

"It's Lieutenant Anderson", the ranking officer reported, a crooked grin appearing on his leathered face. "Move forward Corporal."

The Corporal nodded and swung his horse back to the path winding through the canyon. He lifted his sights to the sky and squinted, the shadowy figure of a man watching him. He shook his head and looked once more, and the shadow was gone. A hiss through the air and a punch to the chest left him breathless. He leaned forward, trying to summon his lungs to work. Shouting around him buzzed in his ears and quickly the ground reached for him. He lay in the soft sand, and soon others joined him. Glassy eyes and breathless bodies settled in the canyon. In the distance the Corporal saw Anderson, nearly upon them. He held out his hand, palm out, to try to stop the Lieutenant, but before long he too fell. Blackness ebbed out the bright sunlight, and slowly his hand dropped to the earth.

Jake shook his head, trying to physically rid himself of the mental image of the Corporal reaching out to him. What a fool he was. His troop had cheered him on the night before, the pretty blonde sitting in his lap by the end of the evening. Drinks flowed, whiskey poured, and beautiful women flitted amongst his soldiers. Late in the night he gave directives for the morning, telling them he would be late and to make their way through Gold Canyon while he tended to soft skin and wavy hair. They grinned and nodded, a silent understanding between them.

And that was the last he saw of them.

Alive.

"Where are you Mr. Anderson?" Ruby's soft voice beside him gently roused him back from the past.

"Nowhere I want to be," Jake admitted. "I'd like a drink," he beckoned the bartender who didn't even ask what he wanted, but grabbed a bottle from the back of the shelf and poured it into a glass.

"It's not even noon yet," Ruby mentioned, an eyebrow raising.

"It's five o'clock somewhere," Jake retorted.

"Where did you go just now?" Ruby pushed, studying his tired look and furrowed brow.

"What about finding your sister?" Jake asked, changing the subject.

Ruby quieted and stared at Jake. "Will you help me find her?"

Jake glanced sideways at her. She didn't belong here. She looked different from the hardened women of the west. She acted differently and talked differently. There was a certain sweetness and innocence to her character. Her skin was still soft and hadn't been weathered by the sun, and her heart was still pure and unspoiled by the ways of the world. She was a breath of fresh air. Her soft brown eyes implored his with genuine concern, and he looked at them and tried not to get lost in their beauty.

"Yeah," he said quietly.

"Thank you," Ruby said, turning towards him on her bar stool, simply waiting.

Jake sighed and scrubbed his hand over his face and pushed his hat up. A voice interceded, startling the only two seated at the bar.

"Lieutenant Anderson here lost his troops in Gold Canyon. An ambush. Anderson here was the only one to survive, isn't that right?" The smooth, condescending voice towered over them. Jake's jaw set and he stiffened in his chair.

Ruby gasped and quickly rose to see the origin of the voice.

"My my," the voice continued, as the man removed his black hat in a gentlemanly gesture. "Who do we have here?"

Ruby cleared her throat and glanced at Jake who neither moved nor acknowledged the man behind him. "I'm Ruby. I only just arrived. Emma is my sister, and I just discovered she is missing." Ruby eyed the man, who had salt-and-pepper colored hair and a neatly trimmed beard.

"Well, that is sad news. I welcome you to town, and yes, I did hear about your sister. Rest assured the Sheriff is looking into every possible angle and we look forward to her safe return," the man said.

Ruby frowned suspiciously. The man's answer sounded rehearsed, as if he had given that small speech one-hundred times over.

"This is the Mayor," Jake informed her. "Since he can't properly introduce himself."

The Mayor's eyes hardened as he stared at the back of Jake Anderson. "I'm Mayor Samuel Carter, but you can call me Samuel," he bowed slightly, his interest now settled back on Ruby, who tried to hide her shiver.

"It's nice to meet you," Ruby offered, deciding she had better stay on the good side of the Mayor. He had power and authority. And she needed to find her sister.

"A word of advice to you ma'am. Skipping about with Mr. Anderson here will only lead to gossip and turmoil in your marriage," said Mayor Carter.

Ruby lifted her chin. It seemed the Mayor knew more about her than he had let on.

"I'm not married yet, and Mr. Anderson here is the first person that...befriended me," Ruby struggled to find the right word. Running into her horse wasn't necessarily *friendly*, and she heard Jake snort.

Mayor Carter plastered a fake smile on his face and placed his hat back on his head. "I do hope you enjoy yourself here. Our town is small, but we have much to offer." He nodded one more time and headed for a table full of men who greeted him with handshakes and laughter. Jane stared at his broad back as he walked away. The mention of her sister seemed to have cut the conversation short, as well as his interest. She plopped back onto the stool, frustrated.

"I'm sorry about your soldiers," Ruby said quietly.

Jake sucked in a long breath. "It's my fault that they're dead." The admission startled Ruby.

"No, it's not," she argued, her voice rising with emotion. "I don't even know you, but I can tell this wasn't your fault. And you still showed up. That's what matters."

Jake was at a loss for words, her reprisal pulling at something in his heart.

"Do you believe in fate? Second chances?" Ruby asked, the passion in her voice still lingering.

Jake only looked at her, sadness and weariness shining in his captivating blue eyes.

"Well, I do," she answered her own question. "I think you and I were meant to find each other today. And that you're meant to help me find my sister. That's your redemption, Jake Anderson. You showed up. You're still here. And this is a chance, here and now, to make something right."

Jake stared at Ruby as a surprising fierceness broke through her quiet demeanor. He didn't have to help her, and well, he didn't even really want to, but something she said pierced his heart, and he knew the answer before verbally saying anything.

Jake only nodded and Ruby gave a small smile.

"Excuse me? I'd like a drink, please," she said to the bartender, who stopped mid-stride and gaped at her. Jake laughed out loud and picked up his own drink. The bartender poured from the same bottle and placed it tentatively in front of Ruby.

"To new alliances," Jake toasted, as their glasses clinked together.

Chapter 4:
The Unexplained Disappearance

"There's firewood on the porch and extra coffee beans in the tin," Tom explained as he threw his saddle bag over his horse. Ruby watched as he tied his bedroll on, unsure of what or how to feel. "I'll be back in a few days' time, hopefully with some cattle."

Ruby nodded, rubbing one arm with her hand. The atmosphere on the ranch was peaceful, but the mood in the house was uncomfortable. Tom still kept Ruby at arm's length, and although somewhat bothered, she was actually relieved. She cared for Tom, but they were more like acquaintances rather than two people who ought to be getting married. There was no talk of weddings or commitment, and Ruby felt the relationship was heading towards an impasse.

Tom finished packing and looked at Ruby over the back of the saddle. He opened his mouth but decided against whatever he was going to say and closed it. He mounted and turned back once more. "Keep your gun on you. No one comes out here uninvited, so if anyone comes down that drive you ready yourself."

Ruby nodded solemnly. Tom looked her over once more, deciding she was fit to take care of herself and the ranch for a short amount of time. Without anything further, he cantered down the fence line and onto the dusty road. Ruby watched him go, a sadness tugging at her heartstrings. She saw them as a mismatch, and she was nearly certain Tom felt the same. Sighing, she headed for the old barn to ready her horse and ride back into town. Tom gave her freedom and asked no questions. She'd caught him watching her more than once, and wondered what he was thinking. She hoped he hadn't heard about Jake, or her sitting in the saloon, but realized that he would find out eventually, since all there was to do in small towns was talk.

Ruby brushed Bonney's soft brown coat and placed the saddle and blanket on her back. She ran back to the house to lock the doors and shut the windows, checking to make sure everything was in its place. The mare nickered at her reentering the barn, and Ruby smiled. "Come on gal, we've got to find Emma."

Bonney picked up the pace down the road and posted a quick trot all the way into town. Jake's horse, Charlie, was tied at the saloon hitching post, and Jane fastened Bonney next to him. She wandered into the saloon, which seemed to always have customers, as the hard-working cowboys took refuge and found something to eat and drink. She saw Jake's back from his spot at the bar, and noticed the room grow quieter after several men grew silent when she entered. The bartender saw her approach and merely nodded, the shock factor of a woman ordering a drink now long gone.

"Mornin' Jake," she greeted, standing beside him.

"Ruby," he said with a nod.

"Do you want to help me?" she asked, getting right to the point of her visit.

Jake nodded, swallowing. "Yes. In fact, Mr. Stavers here has let me in on a bit of information. After a generous tip that is." Jake lifted his glass to the small-framed man with black mustache. He dried the glasses and placed them on the counter, merely glancing Jake's way before returning to his work. "See, Mr. Stavers here watches the stagecoach come and go, being that the drop-off and pickup point is right outside the building here," Jake turned in his stool and pointed out the saloon doors.

Ruby nodded, recalling the night she had arrived.

"And he remembers the day Emma left. Said her light brown hair was popular in town, and was hard to miss, especially on such a beautiful sunny day," said Jake.

Ruby glanced at Mr. Stavers, whose cheeks had flushed. She wondered if he had a fondness for Emma. who was certainly able to attract eyes and men wherever she went, her petite figure hard to miss and even harder not to appreciate.

"He saw her? When? Was she with anyone?" Ruby asked eagerly.

Jake shook his head. "Not with anyone, but Mr. Stavers here did see our lovely Mayor talking to Emma before she departed."

Ruby narrowed her eyes. The Mayor had seemed aloof in his details and information of her sister's sudden disappearance, and yet he had talked to her that very day. It seemed suspicious.

The silence lasted until Ruby broke her train of thought and caught Jake's alluring blue eyes watching her. "Is there more?" she dared to hope.

Jake nodded ever so slightly, his eyes focused on her full pink lips before lifting back up to her eyes. "Rebecca Price joined your sister on her trip. She got in at the last minute, and the Mayor mostly hid the entrance to the stagecoach with his large frame, as if he didn't want anyone to notice Rebecca going on the journey."

Ruby gasped. "But Caroline said she was alone!"

"But maybe Caroline didn't know or couldn't see it, since the Mayor hid things." Jake watched the foot traffic outside start to pick up. A small breeze twisted the dust into swirls, pushing them down the main street.

"I need to talk to Rebecca," Ruby said under her breath. The "spider" woman seethed disdain and irritation, and Ruby dreaded speaking with her. But if she did know anything about Emma, Ruby was hopeful that Rebecca would release that information, even to a "weed" as she had so nicely put it. Ruby sighed.

"*We* also need to talk to Caroline again," Jake corrected. "We need to approach Rebecca at the right angle, not head on, or she won't tell us anything."

"We? So, you are for certain you're going to help me?" asked Ruby eagerly.

Jake sighed and stood. "Maybe I can help make something right out of this. Besides, there's been shady business going on in this town long enough, and I would love to ruffle our dear Mayor's preened feathers." Jake gave Ruby a dirty grin. Ruby chuckled, her shoulders sagging in relief. Outside, a familiar giggle was heard.

"It's far too early for that nonsense," Jake growled, hearing the bubbly laughter.

Ruby laughed at his brooding. "C'mon! She's here now!" Ruby rushed for the swinging saloon doors and flew outside, lifting her hand to shade her view from the blinding sun. The laugh sounded once more, and Ruby followed the sound to her left, where she saw Caroline speaking with two, well-dressed men. Caroline saw Ruby approach and her smile faded slightly.

"Excuse me gentlemen, but our newcomer and I need to catch up!" she dismissed them. They tipped their hats and crossed the main street, heading for the small bank.

"Good morning," Ruby greeted warmly, hoping that kindness would overrule any suspicion Caroline might have about the upcoming inquiry.

"Why, good morning, Ruby. So nice to see you out and about this fine morning." Caroline looked over Ruby's shoulder and made a face. "I see you still have a shadow," she mused. "One you might ought to get rid of," she whispered loudly, so that Jake could hear. Ruby swallowed a laugh.

"Well, Caroline. We were just speaking with... someone, and we have some information about my sister," said Ruby.

Caroline covered her mouth with her hand. "Do tell, dear," she said urging both Ruby and Jake away from the street and into the shadows. She looked excited at the idea of some fresh gossip.

"Well, this person said that they saw Rebecca Price get in the stagecoach at the very last second with my sister," Ruby revealed.

Caroline gasped through her hand. "Who said this?" she demanded.

Jake shook his head. "We can't tell the name of the informant. Just know that they saw it first-hand."

Caroline's eyes widened and looked back and forth between the two. Her reaction was genuine, and both Jake and Ruby realized that Caroline had not known this.

"Well, well, that does spice things up a bit, indeed?" Carlone continued touching her face, mulling over the new information. "You know, come to think of it, she has been seen with quite the new wardrobe as of late. Why, just last week I commented on her emerald-green bonnet. There is nothing like that here, only in Ash City," Caroline thought out loud.

"Which would make sense if Rebecca was in Ash City with Emma," Jake commented.

Caroline nodded gravely. "But you know, Rebecca and Mayor Carter are quite friendly. Her husband died some years ago and the two have been thick as thieves since. The Mayor is wealthy, although no one seems to know where that comes from. We assumed generational. Perhaps an inheritance."

Ruby squinted, more and more pieces forming but nothing quite coming together. She looked over her shoulder and up at Jake, and he, in turn, frowned. She could see the wheels turning over in his mind too. There was just something not quite right about all of this.

"Do you think I should speak with her?" Ruby asked, hoping to keep the information flowing. Caroline's head snapped up.

"With who? Rebecca? Oh no, no, dear, she wouldn't love the idea of a verbal bashing. It's really best to inquire about her with others, not so much directly." Jake bumped Ruby's back with his elbow, in an I-told-you-so gesture. Ruby rolled her eyes. A young woman across the street called to Caroline, and Ruby's hopes deflated.

"Oh, Caroline!" the voice called again. Ruby and Jake watched as a young woman about Ruby's age in a tan bonnet crossed the street, stopping short before a horse and cart nearly ran her over. Ruby recognized her as one of the women she had seen on her first trip to town. She had waved at Ruby and seemed friendly.

"Ruby, Mr. Anderson, this is Mary Johnson. Mary, this is Ruby and Mr. Anderson. Ruby is also a mail-order bride."

"Oh!" Mary exclaimed. "I'm so happy to meet you. I do believe I saw you the other day. Is this your...?" Mary asked meekly, glancing at Jake. Jake snorted.

"No, this is my friend, Jake." Ruby explained, blushing.

Mary tilted her head shyly.

Caroline smiled at her warmly and said, "Mary has interest in our dear Mayor. Now isn't that something!"

Mary's pale cheeks reddened, and Ruby smiled. "Well, it was nice to meet you. Perhaps we could meet for lunch one day?"

"Oh, I'd love that," Mary gushed. "I'm still fairly new, and well, small towns don't often appreciate newcomers," she said quietly, glancing around. Ruby nodded, knowing exactly how she felt.

"Well, you two, I'll be in touch," Caroline winked. Ruby smiled again, feeling like Carolie was on their side. "Come Mary, let's take a stroll, shall we?" Caroline linked her arm in Mary's and the two headed off in the opposite direction. Ruby wondered if the women in this town only strolled the sidewalks and visited with one another, for that was all she had seen them do.

"I can't decide if she will be the fire or the smoke," Jake sighed, watching Caroline shuffle down the wooden boards.

"I know what you mean," Ruby said. "But we know that the Mayor and Rebecca aren't exactly..." Ruby trailed off at the sight of the Sheriff stomping down the street. "He sure looks..."

"Upset." Jake finished her sentence. "Let's have some fun," he winked at her and then stepped out to block the Sherriff's path. Ruby noticed some people on the far side of the street near the bank pointing towards them and whispering.

"Well, if it isn't the two new detectives in town," the Sheriff scoffed, irritated by Jake's intrusion.

"Oh, detectives?" Ruby asked, stepping out from underneath the awning and into the street to join Jake.

"You two have been asking around, and while I appreciate your concern for your sister, this is my investigation," Sheriff Ethan quipped.

Ruby tilted her chin. "And while I appreciate everything you are doing, this is MY sister, and I have every right to ask questions."

Both the Sheriff and Jake snapped their heads in Ruby's direction. Moments of silence passed before the Sheriff sighed and his shoulders relaxed. "Fine. But do so more discreetly. I've already heard twice today that you two are nosing around," he gave Ruby a look.

Ruby nodded quickly, eyeing Jake in the hopes of him keeping his mouth shut. "Deal," she agreed. "Have you heard anything?" Ruby twisted her hands, unable to hide her nervousness. Jake stepped closer to her, his shoulder touching hers.

Sheriff Ethan shook his head but didn't make eye contact.

Jake scoffed, noticing the omission. "You sure about that?" Sheriff Ethan's eyes lifted from the dirt and looked hard at Jake. Ruby stepped forward and gently placed her hand on the Sheriff's broad arm.

"Please," she begged quietly. The Sheriff sighed.

"Keep this under your hats," he advised. Ruby nodded eagerly and Jake leaned forward. "The fill-in stagecoach driver that took your sister to town that day was found dead on the road yesterday outside of Ash City, shot in the chest."

Chapter 5:
Unexpected Love

"Dead?" Ruby repeated.

The Sheriff looked around before he nodded. "We don't have anything to go on. I'm sorry, Ruby. I'll keep investigating Emma's disappearance," he said.

With that, the Sheriff stepped around the two and continued his march down the main street. Ruby could only watch him go. Without another word she walked towards the saloon, with Jake trailing behind her. She untied her mare, Bonney, and mounted, then took off at a run. Jake scrambled to untie his horse, Charlie, still trying to get mounted as he urged the animal to follow.

Ruby tore down the road, and Jake urged his horse on, gaining on her. She took a sharp right, away from the Morgan ranch and cleared a fallen tree, her balance momentarily off-kilter as she grabbed Bonney's reins to steady herself. Jake caught up and pulled on Charlie's reins. One look at Ruby and he knew what was happening. Tears streamed down her face as she tried to turn away from him. Her hands clenched the reins so tightly her knuckles were white, and her arms shook ever so slightly.

"Where are you tearing off to?" Jake asked calmly. Ruby could only shrug, refusing to look at him. "C'mon," he beckoned. "I know a place that brings me peace when I need it. It's a half hour's ride, but it's worth it."

Ruby followed silently, her inner turmoil distracted by the beautiful scenery. The hills grew jagged and stretched toward the sky. Trees provided welcome shade, and green grass filled with wildflowers scattered across the prairie fields. The grass was damp, with the remnants of recent rain still lingering.

Finally, Jake steered them under a large tree and tied his horse loosely. He helped her dismount and Ruby tied her mare in the same manner, allowing them to graze. Ruby had noticed the warmth of his touch when he had helped her off her horse, but quickly discarded the sentiment, trying not to get distracted from the task at hand. The sound of water caught Ruby's attention and she stopped as she saw the creek nearby. The water was clear and flowing freely. They led their horses towards it for a drink.

"It runs nearly year-round," Jake said, amused by the appreciative look on her face that was now free of tears. "It comes down from there," he pointed to the jagged mountain looming in the distance. Closer to the base it's nearly ten feet deep. The further out you go, the more shallow it gets," he explained. Ruby moved forward past him and knelt at the edge, running her fingers through the clear water. She cupped some in her hand, tasted it, and smiled.

"This place is so...peaceful," she murmured. "You come here often?"

Jake lifted his hat up from his brow and put his hands on his hips. "When life gets to be too much, this is where you'll find me."

The admission caught Ruby off guard, and she stood, studying Jake in a new light. He looked back at her, and the silence that lasted wasn't uncomfortable or strained like it was between her and Tom. This was...a non-verbal understanding, and a person that she could relate to, even though they had just become acquainted.

Jake knelt and sat under the largest tree close to the bank. Ruby joined him, not caring if the dirt or water soaked her skirt. The coolness of the damp ground and the relaxing sound of the creek eased her troubled heart. She wished Emma could see this.

"I know this might seem dismissive, but don't worry about your sister. We'll find her. You've got a great team so far- the most gossip-loving woman in town, a handsome cowboy, the Sheriff, and I bet more to come that will help you. Your sister is in the right, and someone else is in the wrong. And there are plenty that will stand up for that." Jake grinned.

Ruby's mouth ticked up in a smile. "Thank you," she said earnestly. "I miss her. And she's not one to go down without a fight."

"Then you're definitely related," Jake chuckled. Ruby threw a few pieces of dirt at him, and he dodged and laughed. Ruby tilted her head to the side, staring, and Jake met her gaze.

"I like this side of Jake Anderson," she admitted. "The Jake Anderson at the bar was kind of different."

Jake scoffed but couldn't hide his smile. "It's harder to be this Jake," he explained, his smile fading a little. "Tell me," he said, changing the subject. "Does Tom know you come to town each day?"

Ruby nodded, the smile now fading from her face. "He does. He gave me a gun. It's in my knapsack," she motioned with her head towards the horses.

"And you're not married?" Jake inquired, his eyes watching the water gently float past.

"No. I'm not sure that's going to happen," she confessed.

Jake looked back at the pretty woman next to him. His silent imploring did not go unnoticed.

"We are just...ugh. I don't know how to explain it. He keeps me at arm's length, but I haven't made any effort to get closer to him. It seems more...like friends. Not romantic in the slightest," Ruby explained.

Jake nodded as though he understood. "Tom has had his heart broken before," he said quietly. "He's not so apt to rush into things I reckon."

"You know what happened?" Ruby asked, sitting up straighter. Jake shook his head.

"Only that she up and left him while he was gone on a cattle drive. Came home to an empty house. She about cleaned him out," said Jake.

"Oh," Ruby let out her breath. "That does explain some things. But there's no feelings there, for either of us. It's complicated," Ruby threw her hands up in the air.

Jake smiled. "Most romantic things are," he agreed, a mischievous look on his face.

"And what about you? No Mrs. Anderson?" Ruby asked, staring at his gorgeous dimples.

Jake shook his head. "I live a hard life and I like my women like I like my cattle. Tame, obedient, and plenty of 'em," he said with a chuckle.

Ruby laughed out loud and threw more dirt. Jake hid behind his hat, his shoulders shaking with silent laughter. When the upbeat conversation died down, the pair sat watching the calming stream.

"I'll have to talk to Tom sooner rather than later. I don't want to lead him on if this match isn't a match at all," Ruby thought out loud.

Jake could only nod. "People are already talking," He shot a sideways glance at her.

She stared at the blue eyes, realizing how easy it was to get lost in them. "Let them talk," she finally said, turning her face back to the water. "Maybe it will distract them from the two *detectives*," she enunciated the last word with a slow grin.

Jake snorted and sat back, taking in the view. For the next hour light banter tossed back and forth, but for the most part, they enjoyed the calming effects of the water. One of the horses snorted, and Jake sighed, watching as the sun began its descent.

"We better get going. Don't want to be here at night when all the thirsty critters come down here," Jake commented.

Ruby didn't need to hear that twice. She stood and beat the wet sand from her skirt the best that she could. The two horses waited patiently, swishing their tails back and forth. Together they mounted and slowly meandered back towards town, pausing at the fork in the road. One side led to town, the other in the direction of Morgan Ranch.

"Are you heading back to the saloon?" Ruby asked.

"Are you done with town today?" Jake replied with a question.

Ruby nodded. "I've had enough for today. I need to think and get some sleep," she answered.

Jake's brow furrowed as a thought popped into his head. "When did the Sheriff say that coachman was found?"

"I think yesterday," Ruby responded, curious as to why he was asking. Realization took hold and she let out a small gasp. "You don't think they'll come for me too, do you?"

Jake didn't answer her question. "People know Emma's sister is here, and they know she's been asking questions," he said calmly. "I think I'll be going with you to your ranch, just to make sure you're safe. Even if I need to talk to Tom."

"He's not there right now. He won't be back for a few days," said Ruby.

Jake nodded. "You know there will be more talk," he winked.

Ruby shrugged and smiled. "Too late for that."

The house and barn appeared in view, as the sun began stretching down towards the hills. The light orange sky faded into blue, and a sliver of a moon appeared, eager to get the night started.

Ruby began to dismount, her legs sore and stiff from riding to and from town each day. Strong hands gripped her waist, and she looked down into the blue eyes that made her heart beat just a little faster. Slowly Jake lowered her to the ground, setting her gently on the dirt. He didn't remove his soft grip, his glance drifting down to her parted lips. The air between them disappeared, and Bonney snorted and shook her head. No words were needed as they both became transfixed by the close proximity of the other. Jake smiled and released her slowly. He glanced at the house behind her.

"I'll stay out here. I'll be under the stars if you need anything." He said as he moved to untie his bedroll, the sunlight fading fast. Ruby took a small step backwards and wrapped her arms around herself, already missing the feel of his hands on her. She nodded and smiled.

"I'll take care of the horses," Jake said softly.

"Thank you for everything today," said Ruby.

Jake tipped his hat, his white teeth and dimples making an appearance. Without anything further, the two parted, their secret smiles hidden beneath the twilight sky.

Chapter 6:
The Town's Dark Secrets

The next morning, Ruby and Jake took their coffee on the porch of Morgan ranch. That's as far as Jake would come. "It ain't right entering a man's house without him in it," he declared, not stepping past the porch. Ruby had to silently agree. It felt odd to have Jake here without Tom, and she wasn't so sure Tom would be happy about it. However, it was only for protection, since the coachman had been found shot on the road to Ash City.

But Ruby didn't feel threatened. She felt like there were bigger things at play, and that the deceased coachman was just someone who knew too much.

Steam rose from their mugs. The mornings were comfortably cool, even though the sun would blaze later. "I can't believe how brisk the mornings are," Ruby mused.

Jake nodded his head. "There'll be frost within the next couple of months, and a light blanket of snow to follow. Nothing like you're probably used to," he added.

"It'll be nice to see less snow," Ruby agreed, finishing her coffee.

"Are you ready to go annoy some townsfolk?" Jake grinned sideways at her. Ruby's heart pounded harder at the mischievous look behind his dimpled grin. She averted her eyes before her face could redden and give her away.

"I sure am," she blushed.

Jake saddled the horses and Ruby cleaned up the kitchen and locked the house and barn. She realized that she neither dreaded nor longed for Tom's arrival. Jake helped her mount Bonney, and the two set out, keeping up a brisk trot all the way.

The sleepy town was just beginning to awaken. Horses and wagons slowly arrived with the day's vegetables and passengers, and the stagecoach was waiting dutifully to take its next load to Ash City. Ruby looked long and hard at it, considering it might have been the last thing her sister had seen.

The saloon was already awake with cowboys coming off the ranches in search of morning sustenance, which was usually fresh biscuits, bacon, and eggs, along with Mr. Staver's famous coffee that he kept brewing at nearly all hours of the day. Jake and Ruby found a hitching post in front of the saloon before it filled up with horses. Bonney and Charlie took a long drink of cold water from the trough provided for them. The bubbly laughter of Caroline Baker drifted down the sidewalks. Ruby wondered if Caroline simply walked up and down the streets of the town each day, gossiping, visiting, and laughing.

Jake grumbled. "I need more coffee. I swear all that woman does every day is talk and irritate me."

Ruby snickered. When Jake threw a look her way, she quickly turned stoic, causing him, in turn, to chuckle.

"C'mon trouble," he beckoned.

Indoors, Mr. Stavers saw Jake and Ruby approach and greeted them with a nod. "We'll have the usual, Stavers. It'll do just fine." Mr. Stavers twirled his mustache and raised one eyebrow, looking from Jake to Ruby. Ruby shrugged and tried to hide the smile tickling her lips.

"Best grub in town here," Jake declared.

After their breakfast arrived, Ruby was pleasantly surprised at how good the food tasted. The biscuits were light and fluffy, and she loaded them up with fresh butter and jam. Jake sipped his coffee and then took a big bite of eggs. "Anything new today, Stavers?" he asked the man when he wandered close to the pair.

Mr. Stavers shook his head. "Well, actually," he thought, toying with his mustache. "Mayor Carter had some fine new horses come in late last night. He's keeping them at his ranch north of town. The bank has some new fixings too. Benches, a new register, and some odds and ends that have appeared."

Laughter nearby caused Jake to roll his eyes. Ruby snorted, trying to hide the sound with her hand.

"Caroline Baker will know exactly what and where," Mr. Stavers commented, wiping a plate with a rag. Ruby assumed that the entire town knew Caroline constantly ran her mouth.

"She and the Mayor both," Jake said quietly, out of hearing range of Mr. Stavers. Ruby nodded, turning her back to the bar and leaning on it, watching the passersby on the sidewalks outside. More men appeared, some dressed in business attire, but most in ranch wear. Dirty chaps, worn boots, and sweaty hats were the staple of this town, and Ruby couldn't help but love it. It was so different here than back home. Had Emma not been missing she would have enjoyed herself more, but sad thoughts of her lost sister squeezed her insides, and her smile faded.

Jake and Ruby watched the townsfolk in silence as they finished their breakfast. After Jake took one final sip of coffee, he set the mug on the bar and left Mr. Stavers a few extra coins. Rebecca shuffled by, not bothering to look in the saloon. She turned her nose up and moved down the sidewalk at a pace that suggested she had business to tend to.

Let's follow her," Ruby whispered. Jake paused a moment, staring at the closeness of her pretty face as it drew him in. Ruby's breath hitched, and she licked her lower lip.

Jake nodded. "Let's go. But stay back aways. There are enough people out and about now."

The pair waited until three men in suits passed by, heading in Rebecca's direction. Jake and Ruby used the three to provide coverage from being easily noticed as they followed the woman. They could still see Rebecca down the street but she could not see them. They watched as she chatted with a few of the shop owners and dipped into the general store for a small bag of something.

Rebecca saw Sheriff Ethan upon exiting and nearly ran to his side. Jake stopped Ruby and pulled her into the general store where they watched the exchange from one of the windows. The Sheriff smiled politely and tipped his hat, and Rebecca continued her talking, smiling sweetly at him.

"That's the fakest smile I've ever seen," Jake scoffed.

"What?" Ruby asked, staring at the Sheriff and Rebecca.

"That woman doesn't know what a genuine smile is," replied Jake.

"Hmm," Ruby mused. Her attention turned to Sheriff Ethan, who crossed his arms as he listened to Rebecca. "He seems...attentive. Perhaps not so much amused," Ruby observed.

"I think you're about right," Jake agreed. "Sheriff Ethan is a pain, but he's a straight shooter. His father was Sheriff before him."

"He's probably a pain to you because you cause him much the same," Ruby quipped, pushing past Jake towards the exit. Jake looked amused, trying to hide his grin. "C'mon *trouble*, she's on the move."

A man shouldered Ruby hard, and she staggered backwards into Jake.

"Hey now. You owe her an apology." Jake demanded.

The man smiled an evil grin and shook his head. "Not in my store. And you two do your snooping elsewhere."

Jake started towards the store owner and Ruby grabbed the sleeve of his shirt. "Not now," she hissed. "Remember my sister," Ruby all but pleaded.

Jake stopped short, heeding Ruby's plea. "You're lucky she's here," he growled, turning his back on the shop owner.

"Did you see that," Ruby whispered, making sure no passersby were listening in.

"What?" he asked.

"The bag that man was holding. It's the same size and color as the one Rebecca has in her hand," Ruby pointed out.

Jake sped up, and Ruby trotted along to keep up with him. They had lost sight of Rebecca but she suddenly appeared before them, with the Mayor enveloping her in a grand hug. Jake pulled Ruby back off the street into an alleyway between two shops.

Ruby gasped. "Look," she said as she elbowed Jake in the side.

Both watched as Rebecca carefully placed the bag in the mayor's vest pocket under his large jacket, perfectly hidden from view.

"Well, I'll be," Jake mused. "We got something going on here."

"Let's go back to the saloon," Ruby urged. "I don't want them to see us out here." Jake led the way through the alley and down the back street. Wagons kicked up dust as they finally rounded the last building and into the swinging doors of the saloon.

"We need to talk to Rebecca," Ruby insisted. "She's up to something and she was the last person seen with my sister!" she said urgently, waving her hand through the air.

"I know, I know," Jake tried to calm her. "But so was the Mayor."

Ruby quieted at that.

"They're handing off something in plain view but hiding it at the same time. It makes no sense," Jake thought out loud, looking around. A few tables of card players and Mr. Stavers were the only souls in the saloon thus far, although the day was still in its beginnings.

"And we have new horses, new fixings around town, items for the bank..." Ruby trailed off. "Where is the money coming from to get all this?"

Jake shook his head. "This town ain't no Ash City. He doesn't have the income to provide all that and buy what he's buying. Those horses are probably a year's salary."

"We need to find out more about him," Ruby said quietly, watching as a tan bonnet strode by the saloon. "And I know how we can do that." She ran across the bar and out the doors, leaving Jake to wonder what she was up to now.

Chapter 7:
A Sister's Bond

"Mary!" Ruby called, with Jake following close behind her.

Mary turned and smiled, ducking to the side of the walkway to avoid the stream of townsfolk bustling about on the last of the summer days.

"Hi, Ruby! How nice to see you again." Mary glanced at the cowboy looming over Ruby's thin figure and blushed.

"You remember Mr. Anderson," Ruby motioned to Jake.

"Jake," he announced with a tip of his hat. Mary smiled and cast her eyes downward.

"Hi Jake," she said shyly, her attention swiveling back to Ruby. "It's so nice to know there are others here that have chosen the same path, so to speak," she gushed, moving closer to Ruby. "Where are you from? Have you married yet?" Mary questioned, eagerness and bright eyes emanating an innocent and naïve persona to the young woman not yet hardened by the west.

"I'm from the northeast, and no, I haven't married yet. It's...complicated," Ruby answered. She was suddenly very aware of Jake's presence. "But Mary, before we go further, I have a few questions for you, if you don't mind? I'm trying to find my sister, Emma. You may have heard something about it?"

Mary's smile faded. "Oh, yes, I'm so sorry about your sister. I do hope you find her. And of course, I'll answer anything, anything to help you," she nodded fervently, the tan bonnet loosening.

Ruby's slender frame hunched with a sigh of relief. "I can't thank you enough." She took Mary's hand and squeezed it.

"We mail-order brides will stick together," Mary reassured, and Ruby felt the puff of warm air from Jake's sigh.

"Well, the questions we have for you are actually about the Mayor," Ruby cringed, hoping Mary wouldn't take back her offer.

"Oh!" Mary couldn't hide her surprise. "What would you like to know about Mayor Carter?"

Ruby started walking, and Jake gave the two women some distance after Ruby shot him a look.

"Well, what's he like? Is he a businessman outside of his official duties?" Ruby asked. "He provides well for the town," she offered, hoping to smooth over some of the blatant questioning.

Mary smiled warmly. "Yes, as a matter of fact, in a few of our outings together, he's shown me his impressive corral of horses. They're the most beautiful creatures, not like the average-looking ones the cowboys ride around here." She gestured to the hitching post outside of the general store.

"Does he plan to sell them?" Ruby asked, dodging some of the passersby.

"Oh, no, he plans to breed and increase his herd. A collection of sorts." Mary moved over to avoid the gaggle of young boys running by.

Ruby looked at Jake over her shoulder. His eyes narrowed and he motioned for her to keep talking.

"I wonder what he needs all those horses for?" Ruby wondered out loud.

Mary smiled once more. "He said a man's worth is tied to his land and to his livestock," she answered simply, still smiling. "Oh! But he and Rebecca Price do venture to Ash City together fairly frequently. They've been such good friends for so long."

Ruby ground her teeth to keep from saying anything that would derail her investigation. She cleared her throat. "I've seen them talking out and about," she agreed, gesturing to the main street.

Mary nodded. "Oh yes, in fact, he helps her financially since her husband died." Mary sighed, as she put a hand over her heart. "He's such a thoughtful, caring man," she gushed. Jake made a sound not far behind. "Oh, and she and your sister were becoming quite acquainted! They had taken several trips to Ash City together."

Ruby tripped over nothing, her heart pounding. Rebecca Price. *What did this woman know?* Jake caught up and gently touched the side of Ruby's arm before pulling back, almost like one would reassure a panicked animal. "Emma hadn't mentioned it. At least some time ago we lost touch. You know, travelling and all," said Ruby.

Mary nodded, her smile fading at the concern tightening Ruby's face. "You should talk to her. Although, she really doesn't invite people over," Mary frowned, her mind working. "She only ever had Emma over actually, and that was quite rare. She lives close to Mayor Carter. He has a pasture and an old barn on their property line. Rebecca said she wanted to repair the barn one day but that hasn't happened just yet. Samuel, I mean Mayor Carter," Mary's face turned red, "says it isn't a priority just now."

"Well, he sounds...like a kind and generous man," Ruby choked out, and Jake chuckled behind her. "Rebecca too, if she was befriending my sister."

Mary absentmindedly agreed, staring out into the busy street. "You should ask Rebecca though. She can tell you more about Emma. In fact, I think she had Emma over for a visit before she disappeared. The Sheriff did talk to her, but Rebecca was cleared of any suspicion," Mary added, glancing back at Ruby. Laughter on the opposite side of the street called to them.

"There's Caroline! I do need to speak with her. Please excuse me." Mary spun to face Ruby like a young teenager asking to go visit with her friends. "Maybe we can do lunch soon?" Mary looked hopeful, and Ruby noticed a small birthmark in the shape of a teardrop on her cheek.

"Of course," Ruby reassured to Mary's delight.

"Wonderful! I rather enjoy the company of Caroline but she's really my only friend here so far. I'm not too social, believe it or not," Mary giggled.

"Well, now you have two," Ruby held up two fingers. She liked Mary, even though she worried the young woman might be conversing with people that might not have her best interests at heart.

Mary all but leapt at Ruby and gave her a hug. "Oh! I'm so glad! You two have fun," she smiled before darting across the street. Jake moved to Ruby's side. Mary and Caroline's cheery greeting drifted over across the street.

"I need to talk to Rebecca. She had Emma in her house!" Ruby hissed, her eyes welling with tears.

Jake walked in front of her, blocking her view of the street. "Oh no you're not. You want to go missing too? Then you'll never find your sister," he reasoned.

Ruby looked up into his angry blue eyes. She sniffled and the heartache she felt for Emma eased ever so slightly. Finally, when Jake refused to move or break eye contact, she dipped her head in agreement.

Ruby heard her name called and Jake rolled his eyes and groaned.

"Ruby!" A woman called, dodging horses and wagons as she crossed to greet the pair. Caroline Baker was alone, and for a moment Ruby wondered where Mary had gone off to.

"Oh! And Mr. Anderson, what a surprise," Caroline said with a hint of sarcasm. "You two are becoming the talk of the town you know," she leaned in to reveal her secrets to Jake and Ruby. "Folks want to know if this," Caroline waved back and forth between them, "is a match."

"Who are these curious folks?" Jake asked, his tone dripping with irritation.

Caroline chuckled and snapped her mouth closed. Ruby couldn't help but smile. This woman sure did know how to lure people's interest with town gossip. Jake huffed and rolled his eyes once more.

"Caroline, it's good to see you," Ruby recovered the conversation. She motioned for the pair to huddle closer and moved towards the window of the barber shop to get out of the way of both foot traffic and hearing distance. "I was just visiting with Mary, and she mentioned that Rebecca Price had Emma over to her home, and that they were becoming friendly."

Caroline's mouth dropped open. "You don't say. Mary mentioned that? Well, yes, I guess she would know, being courted by the Mayor and all." Caroline let her thoughts run out loud, and then glanced at Jane and offered more information. "He and Rebecca Price are friendly. Quite friendly, but not romantic," she added.

"She said that our Mayor," Jake spit out the word, "has quite the collection of horses back at his ranch now, and that he helps Rebecca Price financially."

Caroline pondered this. "Yes, I knew about that, but it seemed in good, moral effort. Only since her husband died many years ago."

"And their homesteads share a boundary? You don't think that's odd for those two to be out there on their own?" Jake pushed.

"Well, to the townsfolk that have been here some time, it's no matter. But yes, I can see how It would look odd to newcomers," she glanced at Ruby who nodded that it did indeed, seem a little odd. "There's that old barn that used to be part of some smuggling thing way back when, before this town existed. Rumor has it that a tunnel runs through it to the general store here," she pointed. "It was used to run moonshine out of town to be sold when it was banned by General.... oh, I can't recall his name," Caroline squinted, trying to recall her history of the wild west town.

"So, let me see here," Jake interjected, seeing Ruby's mouth open and the panic mount in her eyes. "Rebecca Price had Emma over to her home. The last person to see her," he added, leaning forward. Caroline reared her head slightly. "And there's a secret tunnel leading from that property to right here," he pointed to the store. "And you don't think that's suspicious?"

Caroline smoothed her skirt and turned her nose up. "I do indeed think it's quite interesting, Mr. Anderson," she enunciated his name in annoyance, "but she is too elderly to have kidnapped anyone..." Caroline trailed off, her eyes squinting in thought. "If that's what you're implying. And too elderly to have physically done anything, but shrewd enough that she might *know* something," Caroline agreed, looking directly at Ruby.

Ruby sighed and stared off at the town before her. She pictured her sister, young, confident, and daring. Daring enough to start a life somewhere else, seizing a chance to do something for herself for once.

And now she was gone.

Ruby shook her head. Emma had to be alive. She had to. Ruby could feel it. She felt it in the warm breeze and could see it in the stars that twinkled at night. She felt it at the sound of running water in the creek, and in Jake's kind blue eyes watching her, studying her, offering to help. With every horrid thought there was something good that emerged, like Emma was telling her *don't lose hope.*

Ruby straightened and took a deep breath. Rebecca Price would indeed be a challenge, and if she had the backing and support of the town's Mayor, she could be untouchable. Emma could be in Ash City if she went with Rebecca, and a city would be able to cover the tracks of the perpetrators more easily than any small western town could. Ruby watched as two sisters ran in and out of the wagons, playing. The smallest with blonde pigtails darted under the safety of the parked wagon, the older sister with a long chestnut braid squealing with laughter as she tried to catch her younger sibling. A smile pulled at Ruby's lips. She would keep looking for Emma. She would look for her until the end of her days, if that meant finding the truth and finding her sister.

Ruby glanced at Jake and Caroline, internally summoning her courage and what strength she had left. "I need to see that tunnel," she said, barely above a whisper. Two voices tried to dissuade her, but she held up her hand. "I have to know." She waved a hand around, "There is something not right about this. I can feel it. And maybe Emma could too."

Jake sighed and scrubbed his hand over his face. Caroline closed her mouth, at a loss for words about the situation. She too sighed and nodded. After a few moments of silence, her eyes popped open wide and she leaned in, whispering excitedly.

"If you're set on this, I might be able to help, for Emma," she added, her eyes misting. "The owner of the general store is good friends with Rebecca."

Jake squinted his eyes, trying to follow the woman's thought process.

"And the door to this smuggler's tunnel is supposedly a trap door in the floor behind the counter. It leads out to the old barn as you both know now," Caroline stated.

"And where does the 'you help us', part come in?" Jake pushed.

Caroline shot him a scowl. "I'll distract the store owner, and you two can investigate," she smiled, all but clapping her hands at the plan. "You'll have to shut it behind you, of course, but you can walk back when you get to Rebecca's barn."

Ruby snapped her head in Jake's direction, answering before he could. "Let's do it!"

Chapter 8:
Confronting the Shadows

By late morning, the general store was bustling with activity. Flour, lumber, spices, and sugar were just a few of the items readily available. The general store was the lifeline of the town, although some might argue that the saloon fulfilled the needs of the townsfolk instead.

Caroline made her rounds, motioning for Ruby and Jake to look like they were shopping. They split up, waiting for Caroline to summon one of them.

Ruby pretended to admire the spices, picking up each one and putting it back. She glanced around at the crowd and saw the general store owner eyeing Jake with a scowl on his face. She remembered him from earlier in the week, his rudeness outshining any other decent qualities he might have.

Caroline stepped in front of him and tripped, twisting her ankle. With a loud plop she landed on the hardwood floor. Ruby gasped. Caroline waved behind her back at Jake, and he sidled along the outer edges of the store towards the counter. The commotion attracted the entirety of the store's shoppers, since Caroline was well known throughout town. Two men, including the general store owner, helped her stand up while several women fussed over her.

Jake whipped behind the counter and motioned for Ruby who shook her head. He gave her a hard look that said "now" and Ruby slowly eased along the opposite side of the store. Caroline groaned suddenly, and the commotion grew. "Oh, my ankle!" she cried loudly, and started fussing anew.

Ruby ducked quickly behind the counter where Jake hunched down, the trap door already unlatched. Stairs tucked into the darkness awaited them.

"Oh goodness," Ruby grimaced. Jake went down first, waving his hand for her to hurry.

"They're solid," he whispered.

Ruby spun around and climbed down three steps, shutting the door and sealing them into the darkness. Jake fumbled down the stairs, whispering directions up to Ruby. The solid thud of ground echoed quietly throughout the space and Ruby heaved in relief. The voices above them carried on, with Caroline leaning into her role as the injured distraction.

Jake moved in the dark and Ruby waited near the last stair. The smell was old and musty, like damp dirt that hadn't seen fresh air in some time. Ruby wrinkled her nose. Jake knocked something over in the dark and it hit the ground with a loud twang. Ruby cringed and held perfectly still, praying no one above them heard it.

"Oops," Jake whispered sheepishly. "Here," he called softly from somewhere on her right side. A flicker of light appeared, and Jake's figure emerged from the darkness, holding a match that illuminated the cavernous space. Ruby was surprised at the width of the tunnel. At least three men could walk side by side, although in some places the ceiling dipped low. They both would have to duck and watch their heads as they moved about.

Jake found what looked like a makeshift torch with old, burnt cloth around a handle of sorts. He lit the end, and the space grew brighter. "Only problem will be the smoke," he said, grinning.

Ruby nodded, moving closer to the light. "Let's move before they can smell it," she whispered and nudged Jake towards the tunnel. Cautiously, they moved forward, ducking and weaving around low points in the ceiling or points in the walls where rocks jutted into the walking path. Several crates sat in a stack in part of the tunnel that opened wider.

"Look," Ruby said, picking up an old glass bottle with clear liquid still swishing around the insides.

"Old moonshine," Jake announced upon further inspection. "Caroline was right about this place. And look," he pointed at the crates covered in cobwebs.

"What?" asked Ruby.

"The cobwebs down the tunnel are wiped clean," Jake remarked.

Ruby looked at the area with the crates, a musty corner filled with thick cobwebs. Many were stacked up by the walls and reached almost to the ceiling, but she could see where some had been wiped off. A distinctive line cleared down the walls and ceiling like someone had either accidentally or purposefully removed them.

"Looks like we haven't been the latest inhabitants," Ruby whispered, goosebumps rising on her flesh.

"And look," Jake said, reaching for a bottle on the top crate. "No cobwebs here," he pointed at the crate. Ruby inspected it in the firelight. It looked newer than the others, with unsplintered wood and lighter coloring. The other crates had weathered somewhat in the dampness, their wooden sides darkened and split from age. Jake held up two bottles, one from each crate. The bottom crates had light blue glass bottles, commonly used some years ago for storing liquid. Ruby recalled seeing the light blue glass in many stores back home, but as the years passed, clear glass replaced most of the dated blue.

The liquid in the bottle had aged somewhat, and the clear moonshine was tainted with a brown coloring. The bottle from the top crate had clear glass and the liquid contents resembled water. Jake glanced over at Ruby.

"Seems like someone is still running moonshine," Ruby whispered. A thumping noise from down the tunnel made her jump. Jake put his arm around her, and they listened, hearing only the sound of their quiet breathing.

"It's probably just the commotion from the store," he whispered. Ruby leaned back into his warmth, and for a moment neither moved, a pause in time where two bodies and two hearts connected.

Slowly, Jake released her. Ruby turned, following his lead. She studied the floor, the hard dirt refusing to reveal any trace of footprints or disturbance. Still, it was free of cobwebs and clutter, and Ruby decided to believe that this tunnel was indeed being used, and perhaps Emma had been here too.

After a while, Jake and Ruby arrived at a split in the tunnel. "I bet this goes out to the barn," Jake motioned to the right. "Although it's hard to say with all those winding turns." He spun around a few times, staring at each tunnel and the ceiling. Ruby agreed silently. It was hard to determine exactly where they were in the town's underbelly.

"Let's try this one," she motioned to the left.

Jake didn't hesitate, as he led the way. The tunnel was straight and narrow, the sides closing in ever so slightly. Ruby tried not to pay attention to the claustrophobic feeling that grew within her, choosing instead to focus on finding Emma, and the final destination of the tunnel.

After walking a bit, Jake suddenly stopped short, causing Ruby to run into him. "Oof," she staggered backwards. "What is it?

She peered around him, and blinked at the stairs that awaited them, leading upward. Sounds of movement reached them and they both stiffened.

"Seems like we've found the end of the line," Jake said quietly.

"C'mon" Ruby urged, pushing his back.

"Easy there. I'll go first and give you the all-clear, okay?" he said.

"Sounds good," she replied.

Jake started up the steps quietly, his footsteps slow and careful until he reached a door. He unlatched it and pushed, but the door caught on something. He lifted it, momentarily confused.

"It's a rug," he said quietly and stuck his hand through the opening to shove it aside, glancing around. "This is the back storage room of the saloon," he said. Ruby's mouth opened slightly.

"The saloon? Are you sure?" she asked, puzzled.

Jake nodded. He pushed the door open further and awkwardly climbed out, reaching his hand back through the opening for her. She scurried up the stairs and blinked in the daylight. Shelves full of bottles and barrels full of whiskey lined the storage room of the saloon. Commotion in the bar area out front confirmed Jake's suspicions.

"Why would this lead here?" Ruby wondered out loud.

A deep voice answered from the doorway leading to the bar. "Because the saloon was once the hub of the moonshine export."

Jake and Ruby turned quickly, seeing Mayor Carter glaring at them.

"And what, might I ask, are you two doing trespassing through my property?" the Mayor boomed.

"Didn't realize you owned the bar," Jake sneered.

"I own this *town*," Mayor Carter retaliated.

"This is what happens when you put small men in power. Everything goes right to their heads." Jake stood tall and hooked his thumbs in his pockets. Mayor Carter's face reddened with rage.

Ruby sucked in a breath, waiting and hoping that neither of them would draw their gun. She decided to act quickly, thinking of her sister.

"Someone's running moonshine again. Or *still* running?" Ruby questioned.

Mayor Carter shifted his rage towards her, and Jake stepped closer.

"I don't know what you think you saw, or what you think you know, but there is no such illegal activity here," Mayor Carter smirked. "And you two are out of line. I'll have you arrested for—"

"For what? Finding you out? I knew those horses couldn't have come from anything legal." Jake cut in.

The Mayor took a deep breath, his face morphing from rage to a peaceful calm. "My horses were purchased legally, as was anything else I own, not that it is any of your business. I suggest you two find another hobby. Especially you, Ruby. Your future husband will be stricken to hear of his soon-to-be wife's hobbies... and company," he added, looking at Jake.

"We aren't likely to get married," Ruby retorted. "And why was my sister Emma last seen with Rebecca Price...and *you*?"

Mayor Carter's smug smile dropped a little. "She went shopping with my dear friend Rebecca Price in Ash City. What she did there is not known, but if she's anything like her *sister*, she most likely found the company of an ill-mannered cowboy who swept her off her sweet little feet."

Ruby's face reddened and she took a step forward. Jake caught her by the shoulder, and he could feel Ruby shake beneath his hand.

"We will find out the truth," Ruby countered.

The Mayor shrugged. "I suggest, for both your sake's that you find other things to occupy your precious time. It would be a terrible tragedy if two sisters went missing," he said coldly.

Mayor Carter turned without another word, heading towards the saloon. Shouts of greetings echoed throughout, while Jake and Ruby stood in the storage room, trying to collect their wits.

"He's part of this," Jake said quietly, his hand still on Jane's shoulder. "He and Rebecca and maybe the owner of the general store."

Ruby took a few deep breaths and tried to compose herself. I'll find you Emma, she thought to herself. Jake squeezed her shoulder and gently pulled her towards the back door, leading her out of the saloon and into the warm, sunny air outside.

Chapter 9:
Embracing Redemption

Ruby shuffled down the backstreets of town. Jake walked along silently by her side.

"I'll get the horses," he said, leaving her to wait behind the saloon. Ruby used her hand to shield her eyes from the sun that had risen in the sky. Mayor Carter's words stung, but they also confirmed her suspicions. Maybe the Mayor did know more about her sister than he let on, along with Rebecca. Still, the questions outnumbered the answers, and Ruby twisted her hands in frustration. There had to be a way to find out what had happened to Emma. She was determined to figure it out, even if it meant interrogating everyone in town. She had nothing to lose, and everything to gain. Mayor Carter's threat only momentarily rattled Ruby's confidence. She would not give up the search. Emma would have done the same for her.

Jake rounded the corner with Bonney and Charlie. He helped her mount and then motioned for her to follow him. They rode their horses until they reached the street that led to the Morgan Ranch and then headed west towards where both the Mayor and Rebecca's properties were located on the outskirts of town.

Jake rode quietly, and Ruby didn't mind the silence, as each of them were lost in their own thoughts. Jake headed for a large tree down an embankment where he dismounted and tied his horse. Ruby followed suit. The shade offered some comfort, and Ruby plopped down on the ground to relax. Jake knelt beside her, picking up a small stick, absentmindedly breaking it into sections.

"I've got to know what happened to my sister," Ruby said worriedly, the inward pain now trickling outward.

Jake stared at her pretty face contorted with grief and concern. He dropped his head.

"They know something, I'm sure of it. Maybe Emma was being used somehow," she continued.

"And maybe they made her disappear," Jake agreed. His blue eyes were flinty and hard.

"Exactly," Ruby grimaced.

Jake stared at her with his gorgeous blue eyes, and Ruby shifted uncomfortably, trying to stay focused. He opened and shut his mouth twice before finally speaking. "You heard Mayor Carter. He all but threatened you."

"I heard him," Ruby said quietly. "But that doesn't change anything."

"Well, it does for me," Jake stated.

Ruby met his hard gaze with one of her own. "You're not obligated in any fashion to help me, Mr. Anderson. But I will continue with or without you."

"The hell you will. Your sister is gone. You moved out here from across the country, to what? To disappear like she did?" he asked.

Ruby stood quickly and shook her skirt, looking at the cowboy that had run into her on her first week here. "Emma is my flesh and blood. I will never stop searching for her, just as she would've done for me if I was missing. If you've had a change of heart, Jake, then I thank you for your help this far but you're free to go. Emma is my sister, not yours. Perhaps I shouldn't have burdened you with my problem."

Jake rose and took a step towards her, closing the distance between them. She could feel his hot breath on her face, and she stared unflinching up at him.

"I failed my men. They rode to their deaths because of me. You said that maybe this was my redemption, a time to make things right, and I'll do just that. I won't allow another woman to go missing, even if that means I have to stop her to save her," he said, tears glistening in his eyes.

Ruby's mouth dropped open. His words ran through her mind like a train, a mix of emotions accompanying them. He would stop her.

He would stop her to save her.

Understanding slowly made sense of Jake's words. She recognized the past scars that he carried, scars that ran deep and burdened his soul. He lived with a pain that haunted him daily. She reached out for his hand and gently held it.

"I'm sorry about what happened to your troops. No one could have predicted the outcome of that day. Not even you," Ruby said softly.

Jake stepped back, breaking the physical contact as a tear rolled down his cheek. "I should have been there!" he burst out, shoulders heaving as he turned away. "But instead, my selfish actions cost them their lives. Don't think for one second, I don't think about it every day. I won't repeat it now that I have a chance to stop it. You're in too deep, Ruby."

Ruby sighed as she stared out at the grassy fields. She tried to find the words to ease his tortured soul. Yes, she did need his help, but she could see where his heart was. It was troubled, much like hers.

Strong hands gripped her waist and Ruby squealed. Jake threw her over his shoulder and tossed her up on her horse.

"What are you doing?" Ruby yelled.

"Taking you home. You should get married and stay within the safety of the ranch. Tom can and will protect you."

"Jake! Jake, stop it!" she cried.

Jake mounted his horse and grabbed both Charlie and Bonney's reins before Ruby could take control. He led her horse up the embankment and headed back towards the main road, all the while, listening to Ruby protesting. She threatened to dismount, and Jake shot her a dark look. His heart twisted in his body, but the past overshadowed the present, and Jake knew he was making the right decision. It would hurt now, but it would hurt less in the future, especially if something happened to her.

Ruby quieted down after a while, but Jake refused to turn back. He couldn't stand to see her pretty face with anything but happiness on

it. Life was too short for someone so young to suffer so much, as he
well knew. The way the two of them had collided that morning, their
paths crossing, may have meant something. Maybe Ruby was right, that
this was his chance at redemption. Just not the way that she would've
wanted it.

"Look, I know what happened in the past affects the future. My
sister is missing. I came out here for a fresh start and a new life just
like she did, but things have happened that changed my outcome," said
Ruby.

Jake took a deep breath and continued riding. Just in the short time
he had known Ruby, he knew she had a better understanding of him
than anyone. He admired her determination and wit, luring him like
a moth to a flame. He'd met many women before, but none like her.
He could see glimpses of her in her sister Emma, through the brief
conversations they had before she went missing.

"You know I have to do this. Even if you take me back to the ranch
you won't stop me. You have your redemption, and this is mine. My
sister raised us. She would do anything for us. And now it's my time to
repay the favor," Ruby declared.

Jake rode on quietly, her words penetrating his hard shell of steel
and sadness. She was a stubborn one, and realization took hold. She
wouldn't ever stop. He could force her to get married to Tom, but she
might run off. She would do whatever it took to find Emma, just like
he would do anything to make the past right.

"Sorry but there's nothing you can say or do. Love overcomes all,"
Ruby silenced any and all communication after these final words. Jake
lifted his eyes towards the blue sky, counting four clouds amongst the
vastness above him.

Love overcomes all.

Jake halted his horse and stopped Bonney beside him. He could
feel Ruby's eyes on him. The Morgan Ranch was just a little further
down the road, but something in his gut told him to stop. For once

he actually listened. He turned his head sideways to look at her, as he allowed the darkness within to consume him. He was a man tormented by his own mind and haunted with regret, and this woman had appeared out of nowhere, a glimmer of peace in his life. Why, or how, he did not know, but perhaps she had arrived not only for him to help her, but for her to help him. The thought overwhelmed him as he choked back a lump in his throat.

"Hey," Ruby said quietly. "We both can do this. We can't live our lives in the past. We have to move forward." Ruby sniffled and tears trickled down her face. "Even if that means leaving someone behind. That hurts. It hurts so bad, but they would want us to."

Jake closed his eyes for a moment and when he opened them, they were moist and glimmered. Ruby edged Bonney closer and reached over, placing a hand on his arm. "Jake, you're a good man. Despite what others may think or say, I see something different. I see you. The real you."

Moments ticked by and Jake put his hand over Ruby's and held it there. Ruby could feel a slight tremor in his hand. She knew the war that was raging inside of him. Just like the tunnel, a fork in Jake's road had appeared. Ruby knew that whatever he decided, she would support him. She saw the hard shell and tainted reputation that covered a good heart. All he needed was a chance.

Time passed slowly. The two horses rested in the middle of the road without another soul to be seen. Ruby waited patiently, her heart picking up its pace. Whatever Jake decided would alter her course as well. She would miss him, and that revelation both startled her and aggrieved her. There was something about Jake that drew her to him. She felt a connection to his soul. She wondered if he felt it too. Jake kept his hand on hers, staring off into the distance. After some time, he finally spoke.

"What about Tom?" Jake asked.

"I'll talk to Tom," Ruby confirmed. "It's overdue, and it's the right thing to do."

Jake looked at her. "I can't protect you from everything, and if something happens..." he trailed off.

"I asked for your help, not your protection. We're partners in this, if you still choose to be. If you choose differently, I'll be here to support you regardless. It's time to stop torturing yourself. Whatever happens, you are a good man," Ruby said firmly.

Jake's face softened, and he rubbed her hand.

"Don't worry, I won't tell anyone," Ruby grinned. "Your tarnished reputation will live on."

Jake laughed out loud and handed Ruby back her reins. Their eyes met and small smiles appeared on both their faces.

"Where to, boss?" he said, a mischievous grin on his face.

Ruby smiled fully as her heart warmed with happiness and relief. Having Jake's help would indeed be beneficial in finding her sister, but she was happy for a different reason. The future without Jake had seemed bleak and dull. Ruby knew the circumstances upon which she arrived were much different than they were now. She would need to rectify the situation just as Jake was. His strength gave her strength.

Ruby looked to the sky, the sun directly overhead. "Back to town of course," she smiled. "Let's see what else we can stir up."

Jake laughed and shook his head. "A woman after my own heart, "Jake placed his hand over his chest. Together they cantered their horses back in the direction of town.

Chapter 10:
The Final Revelation

Jake and Ruby stopped short of town and dismounted. Jake led the horses through a thicket of dense brush to the trees in the center and tied them out of sight.

"We'll walk from here," he announced. "If we ride into town together, it might tip off the Mayor or Rebecca."

"Then we need to split up as well," Ruby thought out loud. She turned to Jake, who frowned at her. "Come on Jake. If we stroll into town together, it's just going to spark more interest in us. I'll go in first, and then you trail in after a bit. We can reconvene back here at sundown."

"I don't like the sound of that," Jake grunted.

"I don't really like it either, but this is the best course of action for right now. Just don't get in any trouble and I won't either," Ruby smiled.

"I think that's nearly impossible for you," he grinned. "But I do agree that arriving together probably isn't the best idea. Let's split up and see what we can find. But you better meet me here at sundown."

Ruby didn't take it as a threat. Something different reflected in Jake's eyes that replaced the hard flinty stare from earlier. She moved closer to him but stopped herself from reaching out. His eyes scanned her face, searching for something. "I'll meet you here," she agreed.

Ruby strode into town first, casually strolling past the saloon and away from the bulk of the townsfolk. Jake watched from the brush a little down the road. Ruby peered around the corner, a wagon heading towards the west and away from the saloon. All else was quiet on the back roads, the summer sun cooking the town, and its inhabitants seeking refuge indoors. Ruby sidled around the back of the saloon and carefully reached for the door she and Jake had exited from earlier after their encounter with the mayor. The doorknob turned, and Ruby breathed a sigh of relief. Jake would be furious if he knew what she was up to, but Emma was all that mattered now. Her safe return trumped any reason and logic that Ruby had.

Ruby cracked the door open, hearing loud male voices filtering in from the front of the saloon. The noon hour would draw a crowd in search of refreshment and a shady place to rest. The back storage area was empty and quiet. Ruby opened the door, stepped in, and closed the door quietly behind her. She looked around and grabbed some matchbooks and candles from a shelf. She hurried over to the tunnel door, pushed the rug aside, and crept down the dark stairs. She heard Mr. Stavers arguing with a man in the saloon. Once in total darkness, Ruby lit the candle she had grabbed, illuminating the concealed tunnel once more.

She moved quickly, not quite remembering the exact twists and turns. She remembered that the last part of the tunnel journey was straight. After some time, the fork appeared and Ruby ventured left, praying that this tunnel didn't lead back to the general store. Odd sounds echoed in the tunnel, and she ducked behind a large rock embedded in the wall. She snuffed out the candle and listened, trying to quiet her breathing. Moments passed with no further disturbances, so Ruby took another match and relit the candle.

The path narrowed and the ceiling crawled downward. Ruby repeated the word *Emma* over and over, trying to fight the panic rising within her. She pushed past the claustrophobia and feelings of doom, arguing with herself that she had to do this for her sister. Just as the fearfulness rose again, another fork in the tunnel appeared. Ruby looked back and forth, unsure and panicked. She chose the right fork, deciding that if nothing notable appeared she would return and explore the left fork. She hurried now, knowing that she had spent some time underground, and needed to be back by sundown. She didn't want Jake on a rampage and blowing their cover. A shadowy figure took her by surprise and Ruby jumped to the side.

Stairs. The figure was only stairs.

Ruby exhaled and wiped the nervous sweat from her forehead, and slowly went up the stairs, as the candle flickered from the draft seeping in from above. The cold sweat continued to dampen the hair along her hairline. She wiped the pieces stuck to her face. A handle appeared but no latch and Ruby silently cursed. She lifted the handle cautiously, throwing the weight of her shoulder on the enormous trap door, her neck and head bent to the side. She pushed and the door gave way as relief flooded her veins. A dark covering hung over the sides of the door. Ruby reached her free hand out and pulled at the fringe, removing the curtain and shoving it to the side. She poked her head out and realized it was someone's home.

Shelves of books and intricately crafted statues sat dust-free in their places. Ruby froze and strained to hear something, anything. When she decided that the resident wasn't home, she pushed the door further open, reaching the top of the stairs. She wedged a book from a nearby shelf in the door to hold it open just in case she needed to dart back into the tunnel.

Black and white photos of a young woman and man were sprinkled amongst the décor, and Ruby realized she had entered a study. Antiques were polished clean, and artifacts of wonder decorated the space. Ruby stared at the items with admiration. Whoever lived here had an impressive collection.

Softly, she tip-toed across the wooden floor, praying there were no loose, squeaky boards. A large, bulky pile of objects rested in the corner of the study, covered by a white sheet. Ruby crept closer and lifted the sheet. The same style of crates as those in the tunnel lay hidden, concealed by its cover. Through the slats, Ruby saw clear glass bottles full of liquid. She replaced the sheet, knowing exactly what she had found.

She crept out of the study and into a living area with an ornate velvet green couch and gold fringe. A large photo hung proudly on the wall, and Ruby covered her mouth to hide any sound. A young Rebecca Price stared back at her from the photo. Unease seeped into Ruby's body.

"I was the belle of the ball back then," a voice from behind Ruby spoke up.

Ruby whirled, staring into the hardened eyes, pale face, and long black hair of Rebecca.

"Not that I haven't aged well, of course," she smirked, stroking a long piece of hair that dangled over her shoulder. Ruby didn't speak as she tried to gauge her next move.

"Now, the question is, what are you doing here, Ruby?" asked Rececca.

"Simply admiring your artifacts and collections," Ruby quipped, pointing to the other room.

Rebecca smiled but it didn't reach her eyes. "You think you're a smart, witty, little thing, don't you? You have no idea of the problems you just unearthed for yourself. Just like your nosy sister did."

Ruby stepped forward, but Rebecca did not budge. "Where is Emma? You were the last person she was seen with."

Rebecca tilted her head to the side. A dark image on her pale hand caught Ruby's eye, and she noticed a small tattoo of a spider web on Rebecca's hand. Rebecca followed Ruby's line of sight and smiled wider.

"Why get caught in the web when you can spin your own?" she said mysteriously. "You see dear, I had a reputation once. A frail, injured, weak reputation. My late husband saw to that. The townsfolk knew him, and I quickly learned about the type of person he was. When you go through a situation like that, you wonder, how can it be changed?"

Ruby furrowed her brow, heavy waves of fear flooding through her. Jake was right. Rebecca did seem fake. Maybe this was all a ruse, but Ruby wanted nothing to do with the woman, other than to find out what she knew about Emma.

"You're smuggling moonshine," Ruby stated, as the pieces fit together in her head. "You supply the Mayor, and he smuggles it out of town. With the stagecoach." Ruby's eyes widened, as the dusty town, the leering looks, and the stares of disdain all made sense to her now. "The townsfolk are in on it too," she realized out loud.

Rebecca's smile faded. "Only some of them," she admitted. "The rest didn't want to be involved, but they pay for their silence."

"So that's why some businesses flourish and others get table scraps," Ruby reasoned.

Rebecca nodded. "See how smart you are? I'll make you an offer. The same one I made your sister."

Ruby gasped and clenched her fists.

"You join in and assist me with what I need. You will want for nothing here. You can have any man, land, horses, whatever," Rebecca waved her hand through the air. "All I ask is that since you and your sister can't seem to keep your noses in your own business, that you now assist me in *my* business."

"Where is Emma?" Ruby demanded, closing the gap. Rebecca removed her right hand from behind her back, a pistol aimed at Ruby's chest.

"She's out of the way," Rebecca retorted. A dark mahogany chair in the study behind Rebecca caught Ruby's eye. A delicate silk scarf lay over the back of it, a cream and peach scarf that Ruby had seen before.

Rebecca turned slightly, only glancing away for a moment. "Ah yes, the scarf. I thought it too lovely an item for one such as your sister to have, so now it's mine. Just as you are," Rebecca hissed.

"You touch one hair on her head, and you'll join your husband," a male voice growled. Rebecca started and whirled around. Jake appeared, and Ruby darted out of the way, screams of rage following her. She rounded the kitchen and raced back to the study, with Rebecca not far behind. She ran for the chair and grabbed the silk scarf, throwing the chair behind her to block Rebecca. Ruby sprinted towards the tunnel stairs. Jake tried to catch her, but they both landed at the bottom of the staircase.

The trap door slammed shut and latched behind them. Ruby lit the candle she had left on the stairs.

"Run," Jake urged, and they took off, Ruby pumping her arms to keep up with him.

"She'll get to the mayor!" Ruby cried, and Jake gritted his teeth, unsure of what to do.

"I have an idea!" he shouted, and veered left at the second break in the tunnel.

Jake stopped and bent over, trying to catch his breath, and Ruby did the same. "You followed me," she confirmed, heaving.

"Of course. When I saw you disappear behind the saloon, I knew I had to follow you. And aren't you glad I did," Jake grinned, his blue eyes shining in the candlelight.

Ruby snorted. "What will we do? Mayor Carter will have our heads and I'll never find Emma."

"C'mon," Jake urged, beginning to run once more. "There's someone who can help us. Even though he'll never let me live it down," he groaned.

Ruby frowned, her breathing picking up once more. They trotted down the tunnel, slowing when voices were heard from above.

"The general store?" Ruby asked, staring above them.

"Yep. The Sheriff's office is right next to it," said Jake.

"He'll help us?" Ruby looked unsure. Jake couldn't blame her after what they had both heard. The entire town was apparently aware of Rebecca's operation, and he wondered if the Sheriff too had any knowledge of it. And if he did, whose side was he on?

"Well, the Sheriff will probably help *you*," Jake grinned again. "He's a self-righteous clown, but a righteous one, nonetheless. He should do right by you."

The word *should* did not go unnoticed by Ruby.

"It's all we have," she agreed.

Together they burst through the trap door of the general store, surprising the owner, who shouted at them.

Ruby gathered her wits and turned, standing inches from the man's twisted, snarling face. "I know what you get from Rebecca Price, and I know how. And if you had anything to do with Emma's disappearance, you too, will disappear," she threatened, eyes flashing.

The man froze, the stream of slander dead on his tongue. He gaped at her, fear peeking through his anger. Jake raised his eyebrows and smiled, moving aside to let Ruby pass.

Chapter 11:
Choosing Love

Jake and Ruby trotted down the sidewalk, their boots thudding on the old wooden boards. Jake looked around for the Sheriff and then grabbed Ruby's hand and ran for the old painted sign on the building that Sheriff Ethan claimed as his office and the town's holding cells. Whispers and glares caught Ruby's attention as Jake pulled her through the crowds. The sun was finally beginning its downward slide towards the earth, and Ruby felt the pressure to hurry.

As the pair burst into Sheriff Ethan's office, the door clanged loudly against the wooden wall and shuddered back into place.

"Good grief!" Sheriff Ethan exclaimed, whipping his large frame around. He handed a plate of food to a cowboy in the first holding cell, then slammed and locked the bars shut. "Why are you two busting in here like this?"

"Sheriff Ethan, I know this may be hard to believe, but Rebecca Price is smuggling moonshine through the tunnels under this town. The Mayor helps her and together they profit, well, along with some of the store owners here, if they participate and keep her secret," Ruby sputtered, out of breath.

The Sheriff looked at Ruby like she had sprouted another head. He stared hard at her, glancing over to Jake who only nodded.

"What you're accusing here is illegal activity of two of the most prominent people in this town, and although I particularly care for neither of them, nonetheless, innocent is innocent until proven guilty," responded Sheriff Ethan.

"She's telling the truth," Jake spoke up, stepping forward.

Sheriff Ethan narrowed his eyes. "And what about you, Mr. Anderson? You want me to believe you?"

Jake nodded. "We haven't always been on the same side, but I'm telling you, I am here and now telling the truth. You're our last hope," he said, the words struggling to come out.

Sheriff Ethan blinked his eyes several times in shock. He resumed his glancing back and forth, and Ruby and Jake could see the wheels spinning, trying to determine whether or not they were telling tall tales.

"You're obligated to at least look into it," Jake pushed.

Sheriff Ethan hardened his stare. "I'm obligated to find the truth, whatever that might be," he retorted.

"The tunnel leads from the storage room of the saloon to the general store, and then straight to Rebecca Price's house. I ended up there and found this." Ruby pulled the silk scarf from her bosom.

"Why, that's Emma's scarf. She wore that nearly every day," Sheriff Ethan exclaimed, reaching for it. He ran the material over his rough hands and then carefully handed it back. "You followed that tunnel to Rebecca's house?"

"Yes," Ruby stammered. "That's where I found Emma's scarf. We had to rush here because Rebecca's going to alert Mayor Carter that we found out the truth. Emma might be in even greater danger now."

Sheriff Ethan stared at Ruby, determining his course of action. Finally he spoke, and Ruby released the breath she was holding. "You trespassed, both of you," he wagged a finger between them. "I'll deal with that later. However, I'll look into what you've said. Now you two scatter. If what you've said is true, then you'll have stirred up quite the hornet's nest."

"Thank you, Sheriff," both Jake and Ruby echoed.

"Go out the back door and take the back street. I'll be in touch." The Sheriff tipped his hat and strode with purpose out the front door.

"Let's go," Jake grabbed Ruby's hand and pulled her towards the exit. The prisoner ate his food, eyeing the pair but saying nothing.

The cool air of the evening had already settled in and the last rays of the sun peeked over the buildings. Jake led the way, heading in the direction of where the horses were tied when a soft voice calling out stopped them in their tracks.

Peeking out from the alleyway near the barber shop was the round face of Caroline Baker. Jake groaned but headed in her direction, and Ruby tried to hide her smile, trotting to keep up with his long strides.

"There you two are! You sure have caused a commotion. Rebecca is in town demanding that you both be arrested on the grounds of trespassing and smuggling moonshine. The Mayor agrees, of course," said Caroline.

"She *what*?" Jake hollered, clenching his fists.

Ruby reached out and grabbed onto his long sleeve, quieting him.

"Several of the store owners, including the owner of the general store, want you both investigated. They're giving Sheriff Ethan a dreadful time, but he's shaken them loose and galloped off somewhere," Caroline gave them both a worried look.

Ruby's grip on Jake's shirt tightened and he reached over to pat her hand. "The tunnel led straight to the study in Rebecca Price's home," Ruby revealed. Caroline gasped and covered her mouth, shocked at the revelation. "And she had this," Ruby pulled Emma's silk scarf from the top of her dress.

"Oh, my heavens! That's Emma's scarf!" Caroline squeaked. "Oh, my goodness! This is more serious than we thought."

"Where do you think they've taken Emma?" Ruby asked, trying to keep the frustration out of her voice.

"Oh, honey, I don't know. But once Sheriff Ethan is onto something, he won't let it rest. It's best to let him handle this now. But as for you two, you need to lay low. The town is in an uproar and your safety is at risk," said Caroline with genuine concern.

Jake nodded, pulling Ruby closer. Caroline had a tiny smile that Ruby caught a glimpse of before it disappeared.

"Whatever happens will happen quick. Sheriff Ethan is not a patient man," Caroline reached forward and placed a hand on Ruby's arm. "You two make quite the match. And I firmly believe that what has happened here in the short time you arrived, Ruby, is what's best for this town. And for you," she winked at Jake.

"Thank you," Ruby told her, feeling grateful for the help. Jake tipped his hat as Caroline nodded and moved a step backwards, studying both of them before she turned and sauntered back to the main street, acting like nothing had happened.

"Let's keep moving," Jake spoke softly. They headed towards the grassy field near the back roads, trying to keep out of sight. Wagons in the distance approached, but they were too far away to distinguish who the man and woman were disappearing from the dusty street. "Sorry, but we'll have to wade through the brush," Jake apologized.

Ruby smiled at him and followed his lead. "I'm all right," she reassured, pushing sticks away from her body and stepping over holes dug by creatures. Both walked in silence, the weight of their actions beginning to overshadow the need to find the truth.

Bonney and Charlie nickered when they saw them approach. Both horses stood quietly, swishing their tails from side to side. As the last rays of sun settled on the west, Jake leaned over his saddle, arms dangling on the other side. Ruby sighed and sat on the grass, resting her feet.

Jake looked back and watched her. She sat peacefully, wrapping her arms around her knees while she stared at the sunset.

"I'll make a small fire," he offered. Ruby nodded, not quite yet wanting to return to the ranch. People would know where to find her if she did, and she couldn't face Tom, if he had even arrived home yet from the cattle drive. Their relationship was another issue entirely.

The darkness settled upon them, and Ruby warmed her hands by the small fire. They sat in silence for some time, each considering the events that had taken place over the last several days.

"What will we do now?" Ruby asked softly. "I'm not sure we could show our faces in the town, even if Sheriff Ethan makes amends and sets things right."

Jake rubbed a hand over his face and stared at the fire. He watched the flames dance and felt the warmth that spread from them. The fire reminded him of Ruby, for she, too, brought warmth to his life and meaning, something he hadn't felt in years.

"Would it be so awful to start somewhere new? You did travel across the nation to do just that," he responded.

Ruby's shoulders slouched. "I don't know. That move sure took a lot out of me. Although if Emma is never found, I'm not sure I could stay here. But at the same time, this is the last place she was seen, and although my gut tells me to leave, my heart is telling me to stay," she looked at him. "My heart is telling me to stay for more than one reason."

Ruby gulped, knowing that she was putting herself out there. With Emma gone and her heart pulled in different directions, it had settled on two definite things. Number one was her sister. She would search for her until the end of time. Number two was Jake Anderson. Why this brooding, blue-eyed, tormented soul was shoved into her life she would never know. But she sure was thankful for it.

Jake's piercing blue eyes studied her from across the flames. Ruby dared to look at him, hoping and waiting. Once more Jake was presented with a fork in the road, and whatever he chose she would have to accept, even if it meant heartbreak.

Slowly, Jake stood, and Ruby dropped her eyes as her heart fluttered madly within her chest. He moved to stand in front of her and two hands appeared, reaching for her. She placed her hands in his and he pulled her close to him, wrapping his large, calloused hands around her waist, enveloping her in a strong embrace.

"Whatever happens," Jake began, hooking a finger under her chin and lifting it, "I'm with you. We make quite a team." Ruby smiled through tearful eyes, and he gently pressed his lips to hers. The kiss was soft and tender, yet full of the passion they'd waited so long to share. Ruby sighed with pure happiness, the warmth from the fire and his embrace unfolding in her core. Caroline was right. They were a match.

Ruby finally found her voice. "Well, Caroline was right about us," she blushed. Jake groaned at the mention of the name and she giggled.

Thundering hooves in the distance startled them. Jake pulled Ruby behind him and snuffed out the fire. "Wait here," he directed, hunching down and heading towards the edge of the road. Ruby huffed and followed behind him, the moonlight being the only source of illumination. A dark horse appeared carrying a large rider and swerved towards the Morgan Ranch. Jake let out a yell and emerged from the brush, Ruby following. Sheriff Ethan circled back, squinting in the darkness.

"It's Jake Anderson," Jake called to Sheriff Ethan.

"And Ruby," Ruby called out. Jake jumped and spun. "Good grief! You don't listen."

"We're a team," she replied, and Jake's posture softened.

The Sheriff dismounted and walked quickly toward them. Ruby hoped he wasn't there to arrest them and prayed that he had found Emma.

"I was just heading out to Morgan Ranch to find you," he explained. "I followed that tunnel, and you were right about everything. I found all the evidence in Rebecca's house. Both Rebecca and Mayor Carter have been arrested. I've yet to deal with the townsfolk who are benefiting from their little moonshine operation, but that will happen."

The Sheriff glanced at Jake and then Ruby. "I owe you both an apology. I doubted you, only because it seemed so far-fetched. Mayor Carter always explained his wealth away as an inheritance, although there's no records to prove it. Now it all makes sense."

"No apology needed. We had one shot, and we knew you would be the one, if anyone, that could set this mess straight," said Jake.

Sheriff Ethan stood a little straighter, accepting Jake's rare compliment.

"Is there any sign of Emma?" Ruby stepped forward, wringing her hands.

"No ma'am, I'm afraid not," the Sheriff replied. "Both Rebecca and Mayor Carter have clammed up, but it's only a matter of time before they turn on each other. Selfishness rules those types of people, and one will eventually talk. When that happens, you'll be the first to know. Until then, I would lay low until the dust settles. The townsfolk are upset. Anyone involved with their little scheme will most likely leave, if not prosecuted first," he added. Sheriff Ethan tipped his hat to them both and mounted his horse. He gave them one last look and galloped back towards town.

Jake drew Ruby to him and wrapped his arms around her. She rested her head on his chest as they watched the trail of dust from the horse and rider. "Let's stay here tonight and deal with everything on a new day," Ruby suggested.

Jake nodded and kissed the top of her head. "I'll restart the fire. And Ruby?"

"Yes?" Ruby replied, trying to find his beautiful blue eyes in the dark. She breathed him in, the faint musk of sweat and dirt, mixed with a pine-like smell.

"We can go and do whatever we want. Our future is not tied to anything. We're free to decide what we want to do with it, even if we choose to stay," said Jake.

He leaned down and kissed her beneath the sliver of the moon, and Ruby melted into his arms, knowing that he was absolutely right.

Chapter 12:
Embracing the Unknown

Ruby awoke in the early morning light. Birds began their morning songs and flitted in and out of the brush. Ruby snuggled against Jake, and he stirred, the pale orange color in the distance slowly growing to reach the navy-blue remnants of the night. The moments of peace didn't last long before the worried thoughts began running through her mind. They were in a mess. They had caused the upheaval of an entire town, even though it meant revealing its dirty underbelly.

Jake pulled her tighter and nuzzled the side of her neck, and she couldn't help but smile. If only she could find Emma, then the situation wouldn't seem so dire. Ruby didn't much care for the townsfolk, and in a way, felt shunned by them. They had their own agenda. Secrets and deceit paved the town's roads. Ruby wasn't sure she could trust anyone here, even though she had no desire to head back to the northeast.

"What are you thinking?" Jake asked softly in her ear. "I can feel you tensing up."

"I'm thinking about the town, the future, and Emma," Ruby summarized.

Jake smelled her soft brown hair and pushed a strand back from her face. "Well, the future is what we're going to make of it. If you want to stay, we stay. If you want to go, we go."

Ruby shook her head slightly. "It's too early to say for sure. Besides, I need to stay awhile, if only for Emma."

"Would you consider going back to the northeast?" Jake questioned.

"No, I like the west. I think my future, *our* future is here, don't you?" Ruby responded.

Jake breathed a sigh of relief. "Yes, I'm with you. Just as long as it doesn't involve multiple feet of snow."

Ruby chuckled and elbowed him, and Jake grunted through his laughter.

"We need some food and water, and so do the horses," Jake said, as they sat up.

"I'm nervous about going into town," Ruby said.

"Since when do you listen to anything anyone says? Rebecca and Mayor Carter are behind bars, and what I wouldn't give to see that," Jake said boldly.

Ruby sighed and stood, as Jake helped her up by the elbows. "We can't cower in the bushes. Living in fear is no way to live. We need answers about your sister, and we need to see what happens in the aftermath. That all determines our lives," he said.

Ruby tried to hide her smile.

"What?" Jake asked, ducking his head down closer to her.

"Look at you, being the voice of reason." She shoved him playfully.

Jake reared his head and laughed. "Who would have thought, right? Besides, I'll protect us," he said as he patted the gun resting in his holster.

Jake and Ruby untied their horses and mounted them. Ruby stretched her back, stiff from sleeping on the ground. "Stay close," Jake warned. "We don't know what we're exactly walking into."

Ruby nodded and they rode side by side, straight to the front hitching post outside the saloon and tied their horses, who greedily gulped water at the trough. Jake found some hay and gave them each a generous amount. The town was just beginning to awaken, which offered Ruby some confidence. When the townsfolk appeared, she and Jake would already be waiting, the element of surprise on their side. Jake pushed open the saloon doors with Ruby right on his heels. They sat at the bar, turning their chairs sideways to face each other, keeping one eye on the doors. Word would spread soon enough, and Jake wanted them both situated and ready for the masses.

Mr. Stavers appeared from the back and stopped short when he saw them both. With a nod, he wandered over to the freshly brewed coffee and poured two cups. He set the steaming hot mugs in front of Ruby and Jake, his mustache lifting on one side.

"You're going to need these," he said. "I'll be back with some breakfast."

Ruby and Jake glanced at each other. "Could be good, could be bad," Jake shrugged, reaching for the coffee.

"Or a bit of both," Ruby said in a low voice.

Jake nodded once and lifted the steaming brown liquid to his lips. "Remember," he said softly, "what matters is that we make it through this together. You stick by me today and we'll see what happens."

"To the future, wherever that may be," Ruby lifted her coffee mug, tapping it against Jake's.

Cowboys slowly trickled in as the morning droned on. Stares and whispers were aplenty, but Jake eyed each and every one of them into silence. Mr. Stavers remained professional, as he kept busy and away from any drama.

"You two," a gruff voice barked, startling the pair that had dropped their guard. Jake stood, standing several inches above the man with the graying mustache. "I'm going to lose everything because of your meddling!" he hissed, stepping into Jake's space. Ruby stood and Jake moved to stand in front of her. "Don't protect her! She's the reason for all this!" The man reached for something in his pocket just as a voice behind the trio stopped them all.

"Is there a problem here?" questioned Sheriff Ethan as he glared at the gray-haired mustache man desperately trying to compose himself.

"No, of course not, Sheriff," the man said as he gave a dark look in Ruby's direction.

"Then you best move along," Sheriff Ethan responded gruffly. The man skirted around them, darting for the door. The inhabitants of the saloon had gone quiet, the tables nearly full now. "As for the rest of you, these two are free to live here, unharmed and respected. If you disagree, then there's the door," Sheriff Ethan pointed out.

Ruby's lips twitched and Jake tipped his hat. A woman burst through the saloon doors, and the entire bar jumped at the sudden intrusion.

"Oh! Ruby! There you are!" Caroline Baker cried. Both Jake and Sheriff Ethan groaned, and the Sheriff made a quick exit. Ruby saw Mary trailing behind, her face ashen and downcast. Ruby's heart ached for her, knowing that the Mayor's antics would have shown him in a different light from the one Mary had seen.

Ruby stood from her bar stool and Caroline greeted her with a hug. "Oh dear, I was so worried about you two. When Sheriff Ethan arrested Rebecca and the Mayor, I thought for sure you were in harm's way."

"That's something we're trying to avoid." Jake tipped his hat at Caroline and Mary, who only nodded in solemn response. Caroline nodded towards Mary, encouraging Ruby to speak up.

Ruby took a deep breath and moved forward. "Mary, I'm so sorry if I unintentionally caused you pain. That was the very last thing on my mind. Searching for Emma led to.... other things, as you know by now."

Mary nodded and looked up through her tears, wiping her cheeks. "No need to apologize, Ruby. You saved both the town and me from a terrible fate. One that would have been much worse to live through the longer it went on." She summoned a smile through the tears. "We thank you and we'll help in any way we can to find your sister."

Ruby threw her arms around Mary and then Caroline, and the three women shed tears of relief, joy, and heartache.

"Things will change now, and hopefully for the better," Caroline sniffled. "The general store owner is already missing. He just took off and left in the middle of the night, along with a few others. The barber will likely be next, that man who was so irate with you not long ago," Caroline explained, pulling a handkerchief out and dabbing her eyes.

Two men appeared, each dressed in dark suits with gold pocket watches. They nodded their greeting at Caroline and Mary, who bid a tearful but happy farewell, for now.

"You may not know us, but we operate the bank," said the man on the right. "We know that what happened was no easy task, but we wanted to thank you and give you our most sincere gratitude." Jake's eyebrows raised in surprise.

"If you need anything at all to help find your sister, we're more than happy to accommodate," the man on the left spoke up. With curt bows they turned on their heels and departed, disappearing almost as quickly as they had appeared.

Ruby plopped in her chair and downed another cup of coffee. Jake chuckled. "Both good and bad," he mused, lifting his mug to her and talking a sip.

"What will happen to Rebecca and Mayor Carter?" Ruby thought out loud as the noise behind them ramped back up.

"They'll do time," Jake answered simply.

"What about the town?" asked Ruby.

"They'll find a new Mayor. But Rebecca sure doesn't need a replacement," Jake grinned. Ruby swatted at him, smiling.

"This seems...hopeful," Ruby searched for the right word. There were sure to be more irate townsfolk, their world ripped apart to reveal a darkness beneath, but the people that sought them out were grateful. Ruby's face fell. "All that's missing is Emma," she said softly.

Jake set down his mug and reached for her hand. "I'm telling you, the Sheriff is a pain sometimes, but he knows his stuff. Just don't tell him I said that," he pointed at Ruby with a sly grin. Seriousness returned and he leaned in. "Give him some more time. We cracked the egg, and now we're just waiting for the yolk to come running out. Rebecca and the Mayor will turn on each other, like he said, and then you'll have your answers."

Ruby took a deep breath and smiled, as a thought crossed her mind. A gentle breeze drifted into the saloon, and hope returned with it. She squeezed Jake's hand, his blue eyes staring fondly at her.

"Love overcomes all," she said with a smile.

Chapter 13:
Healing Wounds

Lunch came and went, and Jake and Ruby ate at the bar. Mr. Stavers had roast beef sandwiches on the menu for today, and they ate quietly, enjoying the good food. Only one more threat had come in, from a man that had a partial buy-in on the general store. He was promptly escorted outside by Sheriff Ethan, who had taken up a post outside of the saloon for part of the day. A few more grateful townsfolk stopped by to pat Jake on the back and shake Ruby's hand, and Ruby decided that the good was beginning to outweigh the bad.

Ruby glanced back at the saloon doors, swinging in and out with cowboys coming to join a game of cards or enjoy some refreshments. The light faded, and streaks of orange and red appeared in the sky, the beginnings of a magnificent sunset.

Jake rubbed her back, sensing that something was troubling her. He leaned forward to catch her attention and she gave a tiny smile.

"I need to talk to Tom. I know he's home by now," Ruby explained, picking at her nails.

"Do you love him?" Jake asked.

Ruby smiled and shook her head, staring into the blue eyes of the man she did love. "You know I don't," she said.

"I just want you to be sure, that's all," said Jake.

"I'm quite sure, Jake Anderson. I care about Tom. He seems like a gentleman and a genuinely decent person, but I don't love him, and I'm pretty sure he doesn't love me either," Ruby declared.

"How can you tell?" Jake pressed.

"He watches me out of the corner of his eyes when he thinks I'm not aware. He's kind but he keeps his distance, like he's unable or unwilling to try to make a connection," she explained.

Jake sighed and rubbed her arm. "You do need to talk, He needs to hear the truth and once again, you need answers." Ruby nodded and slowly slid down from the bar stool. She was dreading this conversation, but it had to be done. She would lose the place she called home, the man she was supposed to marry, and the security of a new life.

She could have these things with Jake, but it would take time. The journey to healing was long and slow, and Ruby knew that it was just beginning.

"I'll ride with you out to the ranch," Jake said, standing.

Ruby shook her head. "I need to go alone."

"You're not leaving my sight. I'll camp out near the road, away from the house, but you're not getting rid of me. Your sister is still missing, and I can't let anything happen to you," Jake said with determination.

Ruby was too tired to argue. Everything that had happened in the last several days was slowly deteriorating her stamina, both physically and mentally. Jake escorted her through the doors, and the bar quieted as they passed. Ruby could hear some low mumbles and whispers, but she let it go. She had bigger things to concern herself with.

Jake and Ruby rode side by side, letting their horses take a leisurely pace. Both delayed the inevitable, feeling that this conversation was a threat to their very new relationship. Ruby felt that they weren't yet strong enough to face so many trials. They needed time to breathe, and time to reflect and heal. Jake's demons had eased up a bit, but they were still there. Ruby had her own storms to face, including ending things with Tom and trying to find out what had happened to Emma. The waves of despair ebbed and flowed, and the couple experienced moments of pure bliss and peace soon followed by the crash of doubt and hopelessness.

The Morgan ranch appeared, and smoke swirled out of the chimney. Jake pulled up and waited for Ruby's lead. Ruby dismounted and looked up at him, placing her hand on his leg.

"I'll be right out here," Jake reassured her. "Off his property but close enough if you need me."

Ruby didn't say anything as she simply nodded, then patted his leg and headed for the barn to put Bonney away.

"Ruby," he called as she began to walk away. She paused and turned her head. "You're doing the right thing, regardless of the outcome."

Ruby looked back and smiled, and then kept walking, her heart both heavy and light in the same moment. Having Jake nearby was reassuring and boosted her confidence, but facing Tom stifled the fleeting happiness.

She opened the barn door and got Bonney situated, making sure she had water and fresh hay. The horse enjoyed the clean, new straw, happy to be rid of the saddle and bridle. Ruby felt a pang of guilt for keeping Bonney away from home for so long. Sadness pulled at her heart. She would miss her horse.

Ruby took heavy steps up to the porch, and movement startled her, stopping her where she stood. Tom sat in the rocking chair, puffing at a pipe. A fire blazed in the fireplace inside and Ruby saw a pot of food bubbling. More pangs of guilt shredded her resolve, and she sat in the chair next to Tom without a word.

After several minutes of quiet, Ruby spoke first. "How was the drive?" she inquired.

Tom nodded. "Good. We pulled in fifty new cattle and delivered them to Swanson Ranch a day early. We all received a bonus for that."

Ruby smiled, staring out at the sky. The sun had finally set, and velvety blue settled in, the stars already twinkling. "I'm glad. You deserve it."

"I appreciate the sentiment, but why don't we talk about what you really want to talk about," said Tom.

Ruby stiffened at Tom's words but decided to plow forward. "Do you love me?" she asked.

Tom coughed a couple of times, the smoke from his mouth sputtering out in puffs. "I care for you, Ruby, but no, I don't love you. Do you love me?" he countered.

"I think you're a good, kind, hardworking man, and I care for you, but no, I don't love you," Ruby turned her head to look at him. "Can I ask why? From the moment we met you seemed so.... distant."

Tom sighed and leaned forward, placing his elbows on his knees, turning his face to her. "Long ago when I was younger, I got married. She was sweet, slender, stubborn, and hard working. She died of influenza not many years later. I loved her. Young love is naïve, but it can be fierce."

Ruby stopped rocking and studied Tom's weathered but handsome face as he continued. "You're the spitting image of her. When you stepped off that stagecoach, I thought I was looking at a ghost. I should have said something or done something, but shock took over, and I didn't know how to act. I do apologize if you felt ignored. I didn't mean to. I just haven't recovered. I guess I'm just not ready," he sighed.

"It's alright, Tom. It all makes sense now. I appreciate you telling me," said Ruby.

Tom nodded and stared back at the sky, now void of any sunlight. "Word has it that you and Jake Anderson are an item."

Ruby sighed and leaned her head back. "It was not intentional, Tom. It was like a lightning strike. Pure, unplanned disaster. But it morphed into a friendship. That's why I wanted to talk to you. I care for you. I do, but I feel that we aren't a match."

"I feel the same," he reassured. "I heard about the commotion in town. I hope you find your sister." Tom rose and headed for the door. "You're welcome to stay as long as you want."

Ruby smiled. "Thank you, Tom."

"Oh, and Ruby," he continued. "I hope you decide to stay in this town. It's a good place with decent people, especially now that you've chased out the rats." Tom gave her a little grin and closed the door. It opened once more a few seconds later. "And Bonney is yours. She never liked me, but she likes you."

Tears welled in Ruby's eyes as she choked out her thank you.

She rocked back and forth, taking in the view of the black sky dotted with flickers of light. After some time, she headed for the barn and dug out a bedroll. Quietly, she crossed the yard and headed for the road, knowing exactly where she wanted to be. An owl hooted in the distance, eager to rise and shine.

"Where do you think you're going?" a familiar voice emerged from the shadows.

"Where I belong," Ruby retorted.

His hands found her waist and she jumped at the contact. His lips found hers, and together Jake and Ruby held each other in the moonlight.

"He understood," said Ruby.

"I imagine so. From what you said, you both knew," Jake responded.

Ruby nodded in the darkness. "I'll stay with you," she said, reaching for her bedroll on the ground. "I need to be near you tonight. This has all...become so much."

"I got you, darlin'. Whatever you need, I'm here," Jake said with a smile.

Ruby hugged him. "Likewise, Mr. Anderson. Likewise."

Chapter 14:
A Brighter Future

Ruby awoke for the second time in Jake's arms. Her back and neck ached but she didn't move, relishing the closeness and warmth of his body pressed against hers. Jake stirred and his lips found her neck, which he began to nuzzle and kiss until she squealed, "Your lips are cold!"

"I know a way you can help warm them up," he snickered.

"I'm sure you do," Ruby smiled and squirmed, trying to get even closer to him.

Jake kissed her ear. "We need coffee. And some breakfast."

Ruby pushed herself up and sat, blinking the dust from her eyes.

"And we can't keep sleeping like this. We need our own place," Jake continued

Ruby tilted her head towards Jake. "Let's see what we can find out about Emma, and then we can begin making plans."

"Deal." Jake stood and offered his hand. "Let's head into town."

"Tom gave Bonney to me," Ruby mentioned, recalling the conversation from the night before.

"That was a very nice gesture," Jake said. "I want to see if the town has had any change of heart."

Jake helped her mount Bonney and then he quickly mounted Charlie. They meandered toward town, the sky lit with bright sunlight.

"We slept longer today," Ruby said, glancing around. The sound of wagons reached them, the town in full swing.

"Looks like it," Jake agreed.

They wandered past the saloon, and a couple of women waved at them. Both Jake and Ruby nodded in response. The women immediately huddled and the whispers began. A distinguished looking gentleman stopped mid-stride and stared at them. Ruby averted her eyes and turned her head to look at the other side of the street.

"Have you noticed it's some of the well-off people, or at least they appear so, are the ones that give us those evil looks?" Ruby asked.

He turned so she could see his gorgeous blue eyes. "I hadn't thought about it, but that makes sense. We took their cash cow and now they're upset."

"Maybe they'll just leave and find their fortune in Ash City or somewhere else." Ruby said hopefully.

"I reckon so. It'll be too uncomfortable here now that there's no dirty money comin' in, so they'll have to go someplace else," Jake responded.

"Then the town can heal and rebuild," Ruby said quietly. Jake reached across their horses to one of her arms and gently stroked it.

"That's the hope, my dear," he said.

Ruby heard her name called and they halted their horses. After they dismounted, Caroline swooped in for a hug.

"How are you doing?" Caroline asked, holding Ruby at arm's length as she looked at her with concern.

"As well as I can be, I suppose," Ruby answered truthfully, as her face fell. Caroline hugged her tightly once more.

"The Sheriff *will* find her, Ruby. He will. We must keep thinking that," Caroline said kindly. Ruby could only nod in response. Mary floated up behind Caroline.

"Hi Ruby. Hi Mr. Anderson," Mary greeted. "You two have certainly become the talk of the town."

Caroline nodded feverishly. "Oh, yes, in fact Sheriff Ethan is having quite the time smoothing ruffled feathers. He's already threatened arrest twice today and it's not even noon."

"What do you mean?" Jake asked.

"The town is in full out mutiny," Caroline leaned in. Anyone even remotely acquainted with Rebecca's smuggling scheme is being outed by the townsfolk themselves," she smiled. "The situation is rectifying itself. It just needed...revealing." She glanced at Ruby and Jake. "You're becoming quite the town heroes, and as rumor has it, quite a match as well."

Caroline and Mary looked at Ruby, whose cheeks reddened slightly. "Tom and I talked," she confirmed. "We aren't a match, even though he's a good person." She glanced back at Jake. "It seems as though fate had other plans."

"It sure did," Jake confirmed, grinning.

Caroline and Mary clapped their hands in delight. "Oh, people will be delighted!"

"They will? I thought we were... outsiders, at best," Ruby's eyebrows lifted.

"The chaos is settling, dear. Folks need time to see and think for themselves, and now that the facts are coming out, people are having a change of heart."

Ruby looked at Jake, who had wondered that very same sentiment earlier. His smile softened and his blue eyes sparkled with admiration and longing. Ruby felt her temperature rise along with her heart rate. She was surprised at how quickly her feelings had deepened for this man, who not long ago, ran into her horse with his. Never had she thought it would come to this. She looked around the town, noticing people stopping to look. A few more came over to chat. They were folks she'd never seen or spoken to, yet they wanted to express some gratitude.

The town had a different atmosphere, and there was a hopeful feeling in the air. The sun didn't seem as hot, and the streets didn't seem so dusty. Ruby stepped back and leaned on the man that fate had sent crashing into her life, literally. Caroline greeted the oncoming townsfolk and buzzed about with excitement. Jake reached over and stroked her hair, and Ruby leaned into his hand as he brought it to her cheek. A few of the cowboys that approached slapped Jake on the back and shook his hand. Jake seemed a little uncomfortable with the attention, but when Ruby squeezed his hand he relaxed, knowing they had each other to lean on. Always.

"Oh, there's Tom!" Caroline gushed. "Tom! Oh, Tom!" she called. Ruby watched as the man she was supposed to marry nodded his head and grimaced. Ruby couldn't help but laugh. Caroline seemed to have that effect on men in this town.

Ruby followed Tom as he strode down the sidewalk, and their eyes met. He glanced at Jake behind her. He nodded and gave a small smile, then continued on his way. Mary entered her line of sight as Tom walked behind the crowd. Mary looked at him as well. He saw her and tipped his hat, and she blushed and looked away. A chord in Ruby struck, and something dawned on her.

"I'll be right back," she said as she squeezed Jake's hand. "I need to talk to Tom."

Jake didn't argue. He squeezed her hand once more and released her.

"Mary, come with me," Ruby called, grabbing her hand.

"Oh! Ruby! Where are we going?" Mary asked in surprise.

Ruby led Mary to the sidewalk outside of the general store where she intervened before Tom could enter.

"Hello Tom," she said with a tinge of awkwardness. The revelation about what they were was still new and delicate. With time, the situation would cause less heartache and discomfort, but as for now it was still fresh.

"Hello Ruby," Tom nodded his head.

"Tom, this is Mary Johnson, a friend of mine. Mary, this is Tom." Ruby watched the look in Mary's eyes and knew she had made the right call. She glanced at Tom, who seemed to lose himself but recovered quickly. Ruby hid her smile. She knew in her heart of hearts these two could be a match, because Mary had looked at Tom the same way Ruby looked at Jake.

"An honor to meet you, Mary," said Tom with a smile.

"I'll leave you to get acquainted," Ruby said. Tom nodded and directed his attention back to Mary. She could hear him speaking, although she couldn't decipher the exact words.

The crowd around Jake had only grown, and Ruby hesitated, not wanting to migrate through all the people. Jake saw her and moved forward, the group parting and watching him. Ruby tilted her head slightly, wondering why he was charging towards her so.

"Is everything alright?" he asked. Ruby nodded. "Good. Then I think it's time the townsfolk can stop wondering about something."

Ruby looked at him questioningly. Before she knew what was happening, Jake gathered her in his arms. He dipped and kissed her hard, as she squealed in surprise. She melted immediately, seeking more of his warmth and affection. Whoops and hollers came from the onlookers as they cheered, and claps from passersby on the sidewalks of the quiet town assured them that they were indeed the perfect match.

"Jake Anderson," Ruby said, a little breathless. Jake lifted her up. "I swear, I never know what to expect from you," she giggled, her face flushed.

"Likewise, Ruby. Likewise," he chuckled. Ruby laughed out loud and shoved at him.

"Mr. Anderson," a gruff voice beckoned. The pair turned to find Sheriff Ethan standing with an amused look on his face. "You sure know how to put on a show," he mused, trying to hide any sort of smile.

"Well, you know me, Sheriff. And now there's two of us," Jake responded.

"Fantastic," said the Sheriff, as the corner of his lip lifted. "I'm here because I need to speak with you, Jake. I need you to come with me. Ruby don't worry. Jake isn't in any trouble. For once," he added.

Jake's smile faded. "Stay with Caroline until I get back," he said. Ruby nodded, holding on to him tighter.

"I'll have him back by the morning." Sheriff Ethan reassured. "It's best you stay with Caroline this evening," he agreed. Jake looked at Sheriff Ethan. "Precautions," said the Sheriff as he held up his hands. "No harm will come to her. Those that would be of concern to us have already left town or are behind bars."

Jake breathed a sigh of relief. He gently kissed Ruby once more. "I'll be back soon."

Ruby nodded, surprised by the tears that filled her eyes. Jake gently chucked her under the chin, and she giggled.

"Love overcomes all," Jake whispered.

"Love overcomes all," Ruby repeated, watching Jake and the Sheriff mount and canter down the main street and out of sight.

Chapter 15:
A New Journey

Ruby watched as Jake rode off with the Sheriff, and a sinking feeling slowly filled her. The crowd was still chattering about the latest events, so Ruby slipped away and down the street. Wagons trotted in and the town buzzed like a beehive. Ruby eyed the horses tied to the hitching post outside of the saloon and unhitched Bonney, who had been quietly standing and taking a snooze.

Slowly, she mounted and urged Bonney in the direction of Jake and Sheriff Ethan, the dust from their fast pace still settling on the road before her. Jake would be livid, but there was no chance she could just wait around to see what happened.

Ruby rode on, using the dust on the road as her guide. She stayed far enough away that she couldn't hear hoofbeats, knowing they full well couldn't hear her horse. Darkness soon took over the daytime, yet Ruby continued on. She had left her gun in her knapsack at the ranch, and figured her only hope was that she and Bonney could possibly outrun any trouble, but she hoped they wouldn't have to find out.

Curiosity ruled Ruby's thoughts. Her gut told her that Sheriff Ethan was a good, law-abiding man. She held onto that feeling, and convinced herself that Jake was safe with him. Still, she wondered where they were going. After a while, firelight appeared on the horizon and Ruby pulled her horse to a halt. Noise sounded in the distance, and Ruby urged Bonney to walk forward. More light and smoke appeared, as an entire city unfolded before her. *Ash City*, she realized. It had to be.

She picked up her pace, desperate not to lose the two men in the city. She found them, riding down the main street at a trot. She followed more closely, using the wagons and other riders as camouflage. They continued into the city as Ruby tried to focus on Jake. Saloon after saloon greeted her, and women in brightly colored skirts and lipstick to match hung out of the windows of a large building on the corner, waving handkerchiefs at every cowboy riding by.

She pressed on, finding Jake once more up ahead, relief easing her nerves. She halted and moved to the side, watching as the Sheriff and Jake dismounted, drawing pistols. Ruby sat up straighter in her saddle. She too dismounted and tied Bonney outside of a small business that had closed for the night. Sheriff Ethan and Jake stalked down an alley, and Ruby ran to keep up. She peeked around the corner and saw the two men hiding in the shadows. She walked across the alleyway nonchalantly, blending in with the townsfolk heading down the street before doubling back and sidling down the wall.

The moonlight was next to nothing near the wall, and foul smells made Ruby wrinkle her nose. Clanging of bars and chains stopped her in her tracks, and she squinted, trying to make out the Sheriff and Jake, but she could see nothing. Slowly she crept forward, knocking into a barrel resting against the wall with her boot. She froze, hoping the sound wouldn't alert the two men. After a few minutes she moved forward, stepping around the irritating barrel.

"Don't move," a familiar voice growled.

"Hands up," hissed another, very familiar voice. Sheriff Ethan emerged from the darkness, a pistol aimed at Ruby's chest. His eyes widened when he saw her and he immediately dropped the weapon. "What the..." his voice trailed off in confusion.

A dark shadow and familiar hat emerged, and a waft of the pine-scent hit her nose.

"Ruby?" A match lit and blue eyes appeared. "What in the world are you doing here?" Jake asked, grabbing her and squeezing her tight.

"We're a team," Ruby said weakly, seeing the worry and concern in his amazing blue eyes.

The Sheriff chuckled. "You sure are. Jake, I do believe you've met your perfect match," Sheriff Ethan smiled, and Ruby realized this was the first time she had seen him do so. "And may heaven help you." Sheriff Ethan tried to say around his laughter.

Jake held Ruby at arm's length and looked at her with concern. "I'm fine," she said. "What are you two doing here? Is this Ash City?"

Jake nodded. "How did you... you know what, never mind. We can discuss details later." Jake motioned to Sheriff Ethan. "Rebecca and Mayor Carter turned on each other. The Mayor broke first, trying to score a deal before Rebecca could open her mouth. Ruby, we have intel that Emma could be here," said Jake.

Ruby gasped, her hand flying to her mouth. "Well, let's go!" she demanded, urgency ripping at her insides. Jake opened his mouth and she interrupted. "And if you think I'm staying here don't even think about it. I didn't follow you all this way for nothing." She narrowed her eyes at each of the men. They looked at each other and something silent passed between them.

"Fine," the Sheriff agreed. "But you've got to follow our lead. Here," he handed Ruby a pistol. "Don't shoot me in the back."

Ruby huffed and took it. "What is this place?"

"It's a holding place of sorts, unofficially. It's to hold the overflow when the jail is full," the Sheriff answered.

"The perfect place to hide people," Ruby mused. Jake nodded in agreement.

"You bring up the rear," Jake directed.

"Let's go," Sheriff Ethan said.

The trio snuck through the door and down the hall with several hanging lanterns. Chains and bars clanked and commotion from the cells grew louder. "Why can't we just get the jailer to release her if she's here?" Ruby whispered to Jake. He stopped to speak directly in her ear.

"Because Sheriff Ethan here says this operation isn't exactly legal, depending on the day and depending on the city. We're not sure what awaits us." He smelled her hair and Ruby resisted the urge to touch him.

"Okay," she smiled. She continued following behind him, listening for any sounds. The hallway opened up into a massive underbelly, with at least a dozen cells and two jailers who looked like they belonged behind the bars instead of in front of them.

"You two wait here." Sheriff Ethan directed. He emerged from the shadows, his massive figure nearly reaching the ceiling. The two jailers whipped out their pistols and began yelling. Sheriff Ethan held up his hands.

"Now fellas. I hear you have a woman contained here that has no criminal record. She comes with me," said the Sheriff.

"No she ain't," replied one of the jailers.

"That's the one Carter paid us to watch out for," the other jailer said, gripping his pistol tighter. "We're under no circumstances to release anyone from this here holding facility," he recited like he was reading from a book.

"Well, I'm the law, which supersedes any mayor and what he might have paid you to do," Sheriff Ethan replied coolly.

"Don't do it, Burt," the first jailer said gruffly. "You know what happens when people don't listen to Carter."

"Carter is in jail," Jake said, stepping out from the darkness.

The two pistols changed their aim.

"Don't matter," said the obvious leader of the two jailers. "He has people, and they have people. We have orders. Burt," he said, aiming at the Sheriff. A shot rang out, and Sheriff Ethan dove for cover. Ruby watched in horror as the space filled with gunfire and yells. The prisoners rattled objects against the bars and the hollering intensified.

Jake caught a punch to the face and two pistols went flying. Ruby sidled around the wall and grabbed them, her attention distracted by something on the makeshift desk behind the pairs of fighting men. Another shot rang out and the Sheriff punched the first jailer in the face, then a holler let out that made Ruby cringe. She bolted around them, grabbing the large ring of keys off the desk and running until she fell and the earth quickly met her face.

The tang of blood trickled into her mouth, and she lay on the floor trying to recover her breath. The man Sheriff Ethan was fighting held her by the ankle.

"Oh no you don't," he growled, his face cut and bruised. Jake soared through the air and jumped on his back and Ruby kicked him in the face, releasing her ankle.

A soft voice called out to her, and Ruby froze, wondering if she had hit her head harder than she thought.

"Ruby," called the voice weakly. Slowly, Ruby turned her head towards the call. Three separate cells sat hidden to the right, and the soft brown hair and pale face of Emma smiled at her, her hand reaching through the bars. Ruby sobbed and tried to get up. She crawled towards her, tears all but blinding her eyes. Hands reached for her and gripped her tightly, cold metal bars being the only thing now separating them.

"It's you! It's really you!" Ruby cried. Emma smoothed the hair back from her sister's face.

"I knew it would be you. I knew it," said Emma, tears streaming down her cheeks. Ruby released her quickly and shoved key after key into the keyhole until one finally clicked. The door swung open and the sisters embraced. Another shot rang out and they ducked. Ruby grabbed Emma's hand and pulled her towards the hallway.

"Wait!" Emma cried. "We have to release them too!" she pointed at a man and woman in the cell next to hers. "Carter threw them in here," she explained. "They've done nothing wrong."

Ruby vaguely recalled that a man and woman had gone missing a while ago, but she couldn't place who or when it had been. Without hesitation, she ran to their cell, as the pair gripped the bars with white knuckles. The third key on the ring clicked and the door swung open.

"Go down the hall and exit. Wait for us there," said Ruby.

The pair ran and Ruby motioned to Emma, who only crossed her arms and shook her head. Ruby smiled and the sisters ran for the two men. They grabbed each of the jailer's loose pistols and tucked them safely away. Jake had knocked the first jailer unconscious with one final hit to the jaw. Sheriff Ethan dripped with sweat. He grabbed the other jailer and threw him in Emma's former cell and latched the door. The Sheriff leaned over, heaving, and glanced up at the two women.

"Emma," he gasped, tilting his hat. "Mighty fine to see you." Emma laughed, and the sound was sweeter than any music to Ruby, her eyes welling with tears yet again.

"Are you all right?" Jake gasped, pulling Ruby to him.

"Mr. Anderson?" Emma's eyebrows lifted. She darted next to her sister and a large smile appeared. Ruby blushed and winked at Emma.

"Much better now," Ruby replied, wiping a smear of blood from his cheek.

"Emma, we sure are glad to see you," Jake said, grinning. "C'mon. Let's get out of here."

The foursome reached the night air and all breathed a sigh of relief. Two trembling figures emerged, and Sheriff Ethan reached for his pistol that was no longer there. "Rats," he cursed.

"Oh, here," Emma said pulling a pistol from her belt. Ruby followed suit, and the women returned the weapons to Jake and Sheriff Ethan. The men exchanged another glance.

"Who are you?" Jake demanded of the man and woman that had been held prisoner with Emma.

"Why, aren't you Nells and Alex? You went missing awhile ago," Sheriff Ethan exclaimed in surprise and dismay. The two could only nod. "Carter put you here, didn't he?" Again, they only nodded. "Well, he's been arrested, and I dare say no deal will be cut for him. That is, if you two can help testify." A few moments of silence passed.

"We sure will," the man spoke up. The woman nodded feverishly. "We refused to help in Rebecca Price's operation, so she considered us a liability, just like Emma here."

"Only I figured out what she was doing. She lured me to Ash City and that coachman threw me in here," said Emma.

Sheriff Ethan, Jake, and Ruby exchanged looks. The coachman that thew Emma in the holding facility had been found dead on the road to Ash City. Apparently, Rebecca and Mayor Carter thought everyone was a liability.

The Sheriff spoke to Nells and Alex. "Well, you can stay here in Ash City, or you can ride back with us. You're free and the choice is yours."

The pair whispered back and forth until they reached a decision. "We'll go with you," the woman declared.

Sheriff Ethan smiled. "Glad to hear it. Now let's find you some horses."

Within the hour, some horses were purchased and the group was back on the road heading to their small town, away from the bright lights and noise of Ash City. Jake and Ruby rode side by side, bringing up the rear. Emma chatted with them for a while before riding ahead to speak with Sheriff Ethan, Nells and Alex.

Ruby smiled. Her heart that had been in pieces before was now stitched back together. There was nothing more she could possibly want right now, and for once, all seemed right with the world.

"How are you feeling?" Jake whispered, his leg bumping into hers.

"Like I could die a happy woman right now." Ruby chuckled. "How are you feeling Mr. Anderson?"

Jake was quiet for a few moments. "Like I found redemption," he choked out, wiping his eyes with his sleeve. Ruby reached over and squeezed his leg.

"I think we both did," Ruby agreed, watching the sky subtly change its colors. The sun had yet to peek over the hills when they arrived back at the main street. Surprisingly, most of the town was up and awaiting their arrival. Cheers startled the horses and riders. Nells and Alex dismounted first and were greeted by friends. Ruby rode through next and dismounted from Bonney, and Caroline and Mary all but tackled her with hugs. Jake received many handshakes and pats on the back. Sheriff Ethan was declared nothing short of a hero, and the crowd gave him several hearty "hurrahs!"

Emma found her sister and hugged her, their bodies shaking with relief and joy. The sun greeted the town, and the first rays of a new day seemed more promising than ever.

Chapter 16:
One Year Later

"Cheers!" Jake and Ruby lifted their glasses to the sunset. The bonfire roared and the meat sizzled, the aroma of mouth-watering beef filling the air. Ruby turned to admire their new cabin. Jake owned land near town, and after the decision was made to stay, their lives began to change rapidly.

"To many years of prosperity and happiness!" Emma called, and a celebratory chorus echoed throughout the night.

"It's a fine cabin," Sheriff Ethan agreed, slapping Jake on the back.

"Well, it wouldn't have been without all your help. I thank each and every one of you," the Sheriff smiled, something he did much more of these days. Emma approached, her belly round with child.

"My lovely wife," Sheriff Ethan greeted, lifting her hand to kiss it. Emma beamed with happiness, her cheeks rosy and full and her eyes sparkling. Ruby grinned, happy to see the perfect match made between her sister and the Sheriff. Emma had recovered well, although she still had nightmares now and then. Her thin figure had filled out, and emotional scars had started to heal. She had found a new purpose in assisting the headmistress in town with the school.

Since the town meeting, change had been inevitable. Ruby and Jake had opted not to attend, letting Sheriff Ethan relay the details of what had happened, as he gave the townsfolk the choice to leave town or live there peacefully. A quarter of the residents had departed, but those that remained were excited for the small town's future. A church and school building had been erected, along with Jake and Ruby's cabin, and new families arrived weekly, happy to call the town their new home. Several more mail-order brides had also arrived and there had been joyful weddings.

Ruby watched with wonder as more and more women appeared in town. She became a leader of sorts, and assisted local businesses as a bookkeeper, ensuring all funds were legal and proper. She ran a weekly women's study group and found herself called upon for a variety of tasks, like lending a helping hand to those in need, aiding a newcomer, or helping families find work.

The town was blossoming, as the dark current that had stolen the health and wealth was now gone, allowing room for growth and prosperity. A new mayor had yet to be decided upon, and the town's residents seemed to delay the process, perhaps a bit hesitant to fill the role. Jake was asked weekly if he would consider the position, and at first, he refused, but as the months went by, he seemed more open to the idea. Ruby thought he would make a great mayor.

"Hey," a voice brought Ruby back from her daydreams. Emma smiled at her sister. "Penny for your thoughts?"

"I'm just...happy," Ruby gushed. "I never in my wildest dreams thought things would turn out like this."

"You know, there's a saying, that the heartache you experience is nothing compared to the joy that's heading your way," Emma recited.

Ruby took her sister's hand and squeezed. "It was all worth it for this."

Emma looked at her and smiled. "Agreed," she said. Shouts and laughter caught their attention as Tom and Mary kissed. The newlyweds had gotten married just a week prior. Ruby smiled at the scene. Tom looked her way and nodded, and she did the same. Then he returned his gaze to a blushing, smiling Mary who stared at him like the sun set and rose with Tom Morgan.

"We've decided on a name, if it's a girl," Emma whispered. Ruby gasped and leaned in, dying to hear what name her little niece might have. "Emily Ruby," said Emma.

Ruby looked quickly at her sister, whose eyes misted over.

"We decided she needed a family name, one that was strong and courageous. And stubborn," Emma added, laughing.

Ruby let a tear fall. "I love it," she gushed.

"If she's anything like us, she'll be all of those things," Emma said, hugging her sister.

A voice rose above the noise and the sisters released one another with a knowing smile. Caroline Baker made her way through the crowd and hugged each sister.

"Seeing you two makes my heart just ache with happiness!" Caroline sang out. Ruby glanced over at Jake who had heard the voice and was now rolling his eyes. Any male within ten feet of Caroline was slowly retreating. "But I'm here for a reason," she winked. "Dear," she waved Ruby over. "You're needed on your new porch for the dedication."

Ruby sighed and smiled, shaking her head. She didn't like a big fuss, and preferred the attention to go to Emma, who was pregnant with the first child the town had seen in some time, or Tom and Mary, the newlyweds. Still, the townsfolk were relentless, and she saw the Sheriff and a few cowboy friends of Jake pushing him forward as well.

Jake shook his head, laughing, as he reached for Ruby's hand. They climbed up the two wooden stairs to their porch and Ruby looked around them, hardly believing this home was now theirs.

Ruby looked at her perfect match standing beside her. He had come such a long way over the last year. He was warm and welcoming, and the hard edge was a thing of the past, although he still did have a mouth on him. Listening to Sheriff Ethan and Jake's arguments was quite entertaining. They eventually would always put their differences aside, but still enjoyed vexing one another.

Jake grinned that mischievous grin with his amazing dimples and Ruby's heart melted. He lifted her hand and kissed it, and a few whistles from the crowd sounded through the air. Ruby laughed, and dropped her head, embarrassed by the attention. She only wanted attention from one man, and he had eyes bluer than the sunniest sky. He was her rock, her pillar, her best friend, and the love of her life. Her soul had felt a connection with him back when they had first met, recognizing its perfect match. She glanced over to find him watching her with that look of admiration and love in his eyes that he got whenever he looked at her, and she smiled at him as her heart swelled with love and happiness.

"You look beautiful, sweetheart," Jake whispered, pushing his hat up to let her see him waggling his eyebrows. Ruby giggled and blushed deeper.

"Ruby, Ruby, dear! Face the cabin so we can begin!" Caroline called out. Jake winked at Ruby as they stepped aside. The crowd behind them quieted down and Caroline began with a few words. "Friends, we gather here today to celebrate the new home of Ruby and Jake." Cheers and hollers interrupted Caroline, who hushed them like a mother hen. "To see a life and home built on love, on a foundation built by sweat and hard work, and a future bright and joyous!" Clapping ensued and Ruby wondered how long she'd have to stand here feeling self-conscious. She would rather celebrate quietly with just a few friends.

A hush came over the crowd and steps approached behind her. "Welcome home, Mrs. Anderson," Jake said, his voice loud and clear. Ruby turned to look at Jake and was startled to find him on one knee. Caroline winked at her, and Ruby smiled. Emma and Sheriff Ethan placed their arms around each other and hugged tightly as they watched.

"Ruby, you are the love of my life and my soul mate. I'm a changed man because of you, and I'll forever be grateful that you took a chance on this old cowboy and didn't give up." Jake paused to wipe the tears from his eyes. "You've made my life complete and brought redemption to this wandering soul of mine. I love you more with every breath I take, and I want to spend the rest of my life making you feel as special and cherished as you deserve. Will you do me the biggest honor of my life and marry me?" Jake lifted a stunning gold ring, the sunlight dancing behind it.

Ruby was unable to stop the tears from falling. "Of course!" she cried happily.

The cheers of the townsfolk drowned out her cries. Jake placed the ring on her finger, then picked her up and twirled her around.

"Love overcomes all," he whispered in her ear as he dipped and kissed her. A year ago, they had both been so lost. Neither could have imagined the happiness that lay ahead and the feeling of peace within their souls that fate would have in store for them, and they looked forward to a bright future ahead.

If you enjoyed this book, please take a few moments to write a review of it. Thank you!

Milton Keynes UK
Ingram Content Group UK Ltd.
UKHW042310160224
437951UK00004B/369